**Peyton looked down at the package. There was something printed on it in black marker.**

"'Gunther's Scuba Shop, Rock River,'" she read the words out loud.

Spark sniffed the parcel absentmindedly, then wandered toward the bow of the boat. Peyton blinked. "Whatever this is, I don't think it's drugs."

Asher's eyes widened. "Are you sure?"

"Spark didn't alert," she said, "and I trust Spark's detection skills better than any drug-detection test."

Spark barked suddenly and urgently. A motor roared to the right. It sounded small and aggressive. She turned to see a figure clad in a wet suit speed around the corner standing on a Jet Ski. Goggles covered his face.

The figure raised his arm. There was a gun in his hand.

He aimed it at them and opened fire.

\* \* \*

*Pacific Northwest K-9 Unit*

**Maggie K. Black** is an award-winning journalist and romantic suspense author with an insatiable love of traveling the world. She has lived in the American South, Europe and the Middle East. She now makes her home in Canada with her history-teacher husband, their two beautiful girls and a small but mighty dog. Maggie enjoys connecting with her readers at maggiekblack.com.

### Books by Maggie K. Black

### Love Inspired Suspense

*Undercover Protection*
*Surviving the Wilderness*
*Her Forgotten Life*
*Cold Case Chase*

### *Pacific Northwest K-9 Unit*

*Undercover Operation*

### *Rocky Mountain K-9 Unit*

*Explosive Revenge*

### *Protected Identities*

*Christmas Witness Protection*
*Runaway Witness*
*Witness Protection Unraveled*
*Christmas Witness Conspiracy*

Visit the Author Profile page at LoveInspired.com for more titles.

# UNDERCOVER OPERATION

## MAGGIE K. BLACK

**LOVE INSPIRED** SUSPENSE
INSPIRATIONAL ROMANCE

Special thanks and acknowledgment are given to Maggie K. Black
for her contribution to the Pacific Northwest K-9 Unit miniseries.

# LOVE INSPIRED® SUSPENSE
### INSPIRATIONAL ROMANCE

Recycling programs
for this product may
not exist in your area.

ISBN-13: 978-1-335-59906-3

Undercover Operation

For questions and comments about the quality of this book, please contact us
at CustomerService@Harlequin.com.

Love Inspired
22 Adelaide St. West, 41st Floor
Toronto, Ontario M5H 4E3, Canada
www.LoveInspired.com

Printed in U.S.A.

Trust in the Lord with all thine heart;
and lean not unto thine own understanding.
—*Proverbs* 3:5

For Gwen
the honorary grandma to every child in our church
and all those who go out of their way to love others

# ONE

Officer Asher Gilmore of the Pacific Northwest K-9 Unit sauntered down the Rock River boardwalk toward the marina and pier with what he hoped looked like the swagger of a man who was new in town and looking to make friends with the wrong kind of people. The tourist area was bustling, with souvenir stalls and food trucks, along with busking musicians, caricaturists and, above all, tour boat operators urging those who passed to come and experience the glorious Pacific waters from the decks of their boats before the weather turned cold.

It was Asher's first day of a new undercover assignment as "Dan Johnson"—a Canadian boat operator, newly married to a beautiful American wife, and someone who wasn't opposed to making a little extra cash by running drugs across the border. He'd grown a beard for the operation and darkened his light brown hair. Mirrored sunglasses hid his eyes to disguise the way he scanned the scene for signs of trouble. His K-9 partner, Spark, an English springer spaniel, walked by his side and was undercover too, with a bright red bandana tied around his neck instead of his usual K-9 vest. On the outside Asher knew he looked confident, maybe even a little cocky. But under the surface he could feel the tension building at the back of his neck like someone had wrapped a thick rubber band around the top of his spine.

He and Spark were used to tackling cases solo or with their fellow officers. But this time they'd be working with the unit's lead K-9 trainer. Peyton Burns, posing as his wife, "Merry," was waiting for them at the boat. Asher let out a long breath. He had a whole bunch of complicated feelings about the fact the PNK9's chief, Donovan Fanelli, had decided that Asher and Peyton should go undercover as a pair of happy newlyweds. In June, three precious bloodhound puppies had been stolen from the PNK9 training center. Peyton had not only been devastated, she'd been determined to find them and bring them home safely. Now they finally had a lead that the stolen pups might be somewhere in the area, and Chief Fanelli had wanted Peyton to be on the mission. As she'd been training Ranger, Agent and Chief, she knew the pups better than anyone. Plus, Peyton was so devoted to her job that she'd even graduated from the police academy and a K-9 training program in order to more fully understand what the dogs and officers needed. Fanelli had felt she brought invaluable skills to this investigation.

But although Peyton would never know it, Asher had actually initially argued against having her with him on the mission. With his own half sister, Mara, currently on the run, a prime suspect in the double homicide of her ex-boyfriend and his new girlfriend, Asher didn't exactly have the best track record for keeping the women in his life safe. The need to protect the beautiful trainer from harm was an unwanted complication and distraction he couldn't afford.

He felt his K-9 partner tug at his leash. Asher looked down. The black-and-white springer spaniel glanced up at Asher and swished his tail to let him know that his keen nose detected drugs in the area. Asher ran a hand over the dog's head to thank him for letting him know. He almost felt sorry for the pup. The Pacific Ocean's Salish Sea that ran between the United States and Canadian border was a hotbed for the illegal cross-border drug smuggling trade. Asher wouldn't be surprised if his partner's highly trained nose was picking up all kinds of suspicious smells right now. He knew a little something himself about sensing that something wrong was going down but being unable to do a fool thing about it.

Any drug smugglers they managed to bust and put away on this mission would be a happy bonus. Their focus was finding those three stolen bloodhound puppies.

The smell of hot cheese, bacon grease and decent coffee wafted toward him from the Olympic Snacks and Sandwiches food truck on his right. He aimed for it, trying not to look too eager, and joined the end of the line. Two weeks earlier he and Spark had been searching for the puppies in a network of caves in North Cascades National Park with his PNK9 colleagues. The search hadn't turned up any puppies. But they had found dog fur and evidence the bloodhounds had been in the caves recently. They'd also found a crumpled receipt for the very food truck Asher was now striding toward. What's more, Spark had detected drug residue on it, solidifying the theory that whoever had taken the puppies was involved in the drug trade.

Someone involved in the theft of the puppies had been in this area, and maybe even stood in this line, not more than a couple of weeks ago. But did that mean that whoever stole the bloodhounds was somehow linked to the people working at this food truck? Or just that someone linked with the theft had been in this area? He didn't know. But either way he was here to find out.

He glanced around. "Is the line always this slow?" he muttered, to no one in particular.

"Yeah, pretty much, but the food's worth it." A voice came from behind him. He looked back to see a grizzled man with calloused hands who smelled of cigarettes and salt water. The man looked down at Spark and smiled. "That's a beautiful dog you got there."

Asher felt the hint of a genuine smile cross his face.

"Thanks," Asher said and scratched his beard. "Smart as a whip too. But you can thank my wife for that."

Funny how heavily and uneasily the word "wife" sat on his tongue.

"Is that so?" the man asked. He reached out and scratched Spark behind the ears. Spark wagged his tail approvingly.

"Oh, yeah," Asher said. "She taught him every trick he knows. If it was up to her, we'd have a dozen more of them."

The line moved forward. Chief Fanelli had once told him that the best undercover stories contained a small kernel of truth. Spark was absolutely crazy about Peyton. Truth was Asher was hard-pressed to think of a K-9 trainer and all-around person he admired more. It wouldn't exactly be hard to pretend he cared about her.

But it had been five years since Asher's disastrously failed attempt at a marriage had ended in divorce. That relationship hadn't even lasted two years. His wife, Lucie, had traveled a lot for work—along with a colleague who Asher later discovered she'd had an affair with. It had hurt him deep, in a way he couldn't even explain because his own dad had done the exact same thing to his mom. Asher had been ten when he'd discovered his dad had cheated on his mom. Then his father had left them to marry Mara's mother and start a new family without him.

Still, he'd been willing to forgive Lucie and work past it. Instead, Lucie had accused him of being controlling and paranoid. She'd practically told him that he was unlovable. She was married to that same colleague now.

Leaving Asher with the knowledge he didn't have it in him to be anybody's husband.

And now his boss was saddling him with a make-believe wife?

*Lord*, he prayed silently. *I'm really gonna need Your help with this one.*

"What can I get you?" a woman's voice asked. Asher looked up to realize he'd been so lost in thought he hadn't even noticed that he'd reached the front of the line. The woman behind the counter had a friendly face and brown curly hair with gray growing in at the roots. Asher always made it a point to notice everything while on a case. The smallest detail could come in handy later.

"Two coffees, please," Asher said. "Large. And if you can throw some cream and sugar in a bag on the side that would be appreciated. My wife is the kind of gal who knows exactly what she wants, and if I try to mix it myself I might get it wrong."

The woman chuckled.

"Smart man," she said. "How long you been married?"

"Few weeks," Asher said. "Hopefully it hasn't been long enough for me to make too many mistakes yet."

The woman laughed again. Then she nodded at the large red maple leaf pin on his lapel.

"You Canadian?" she asked and poured two steaming hot coffees into takeaway cups.

"Yes, ma'am," he said. "My wife's American. We've got a really sweet boat we bought from her cousin, and have been running boat tours off the coast of Vancouver for the past couple years. We're looking at expanding into some whale watching and cross-border trips. So figured we'd come down for a few days, take a look around and try to rustle up some business."

He slid a business card across the counter with the names Dan and Merry Johnson and the phone number, social media and website the PNK9's tech expert had set up for their cover story.

"Feel free to pass my name along to anyone you know who could use the help of a good boat to transport their stuff around," Asher added. He'd been dropping the same message around town since they'd arrived the night before. "We've got our ways to get back and forth across the border without a hassle, and I'm never opposed to making a bit of extra money on the side. You know what I mean?"

The woman nodded mildly as if she didn't and instead just suggested he get a homemade pastry to go with his coffee. Asher wondered if it would look suspicious if he'd lined up this long and only ordered coffee. After all, he still didn't know what it meant that a receipt for this food truck along with drug residue had been found while the team had been searching caves

for the stolen puppies. He ordered six different pastries to be on the safe side and balanced
them on a cardboard tray with the two coffees
and a small paper bag of cream and sugars.

Then Asher turned back and caught the eye
of the same man who'd complimented Spark a
few moments earlier. The man's smile had disappeared, leaving a scowl in its place. Asher
had zero doubt that the man had not only overheard what Asher had said, but that he'd understood what Asher meant by it.

Was he a criminal? Or somebody who didn't
much like knowing there were criminals running drugs in his town? Either way, Asher
wasn't here to make friends, and it seemed he
was already succeeding in attracting the wrong
type of attention.

Now to keep tossing more bait in the water
until hopefully he reeled in something big.

Gray clouds hovered at the edge of the horizon as he and Spark walked through the marina toward his boat. October in Washington
State could get downright chilly. Tourist season would be wrapping up within days, so Dan
and Merry's cover story was that they were
scouting things out now to launch their business in earnest when the weather warmed up in
the spring. The day's forecast hadn't actually
predicted rain, just a faint and gloomy drizzle

later in the afternoon that would keep most people from wanting to go outside. Thankfully nothing but clear skies and sunshine was expected for tomorrow morning, before the storm came back later that day.

He rounded a corner, walked down a gangway and along a long dock toward the slip where Peyton would be waiting for him. The forty-three-foot yacht was sleek with wraparound seats in the bow, a small but well-equipped galley below deck and a large U-shaped seating area in the back that opened to a large swim platform. A nice boat but over a decade old, which Asher thought suited their cover story. It was officially the property of the United States government after having been seized in a criminal raid off the coast of San Diego a few years ago. They'd loaned it to the PNK9 for their undercover operation. It had been given a fresh yellow paint job and hull identification number for the mission, along with a new name—*The Mixed Blessing*.

The boat came into view. Asher's footsteps froze and a sudden flash of heat rose to the back of his neck. Two rough-looking louts seemed to be hassling Peyton. She was standing on the dock just beside the boat, and the two men had hemmed her in on either side. The man with his back to Asher wore a backward baseball cap and was so thin that his clothes seemed to wilt on his skinny frame. But the other was built like a grizzly, with a thick black beard, and he'd braced one large paw against the side of their boat, while he leaned toward Peyton like someone looming over a fence looking to see what he could steal.

Spark growled softly almost under his breath. The dog's tail swished aggressively. Asher wasn't the only one who had a bad feeling about these guys. His footsteps quickened. Peyton looked up, and even with the combination of a blond wig, baseball cap and tinted sunglasses obscuring her features, somehow he knew that her eyes were locked on his face.

"Danny!" she shouted. "Honey!"

Peyton slipped out from between the men and ran a few steps down the dock toward him. A huge smile crossed her face, as if he really was her beloved new husband. As she reached for him, he instinctively set the coffees and pastries down, his arms parted too, and she tumbled into his embrace and wrapped her arms around his neck. The smell of honeysuckle and gardenias filled his senses. Peyton's hug felt so strange and yet so familiar all at the same time. Her mouth moved past his ear. "We've got a lead," she whispered. "They want our help transporting a package."

She started to pull back, but his hands lingered on her arms.

"Are you okay?" he whispered back.

They were standing so close he could see her eyes blink behind her tinted lenses.

"Yeah, of course I'm fine," she said. "Are you?"

And that's when he realized he wasn't. Between the sight of those two men leering at her, to the feel of her arms wrapped around him, his heart was now beating a million miles an hour faster than it had any right to be. They finally had criminals wanting to bring them into their drug operation.

And if Asher didn't get ahold of his emotions—and quickly—he could blow the entire mission.

Peyton watched as Asher stepped back and then he hesitated. She'd felt like she'd been treading water for the last few minutes, trying to keep the thugs from leaving while also refusing their not-too-subtle suggestion that they'd like to take a look around the boat. Although she'd done the same training as the PNK9 officers, she'd never worked as a cop herself and this was her first time on the front line of an active case. She picked up the tray of coffees and silently prayed she wouldn't let Asher down.

But just as quickly as Asher had seemingly frozen, he got himself unstuck again. He pressed the end of Spark's leash into her hand and then sauntered down the pier with the grin of a man who was happy to see them for now but who they wouldn't want to mess with on a bad day.

"Hello. Dan Johnson," he said. He ran his hand down the side of his jeans as if he was about to extend it for a handshake, but then crossed his arms instead as if something had made him think better of it. "What can I do for you?"

She watched as the men eyed Asher. Was it her imagination or did the large one notice the slight bulge above Asher's ankle where his untraceable gun was holstered?

"We heard you might be crossing over to Canada today." The large man spoke first. "Wondered if you'd be free to pick something up for us and bring it back."

"For a friend of ours," the thinner man added.

Asher's jaw moved like he was rolling his words around before saying them.

"Could do," Asher said. "Doesn't look like much of a day for tourists. So, the wife and I might go get some errands done." He glanced from one man to the other. "What are we talking about?"

The larger of the two men gave him a set of coordinates just off the coast of Victoria, British Columbia. So far, he was the one who'd done most of the talking, and Peyton got the impression that he was the one in charge. But she wasn't sure if that was an official thing or just that he had the more dominant personality.

"A guy will meet you there," the man went on. "He'll hand you a package and give you the address to take it to. When you drop the package off, the person you deliver it to will give you a hundred bucks."

"What kind of boat?" Asher asked.

"Zodiac-style," he said. "Inflatable one with the motor on the back. You know what that is?"

Asher snorted. "Yeah, I know what kind of boat that is. And does this guy have a name?" The men didn't answer. "Who do I tell them sent me?"

"Don't you worry about that," the larger man said. "We're a need-to-know operation."

Asher's eyes rolled. It was incredible how seamlessly he'd stepped into the role of Dan Johnson. Peyton ran her hand over the back of Spark's head and stroked the dog's silky ears. As she brushed her hand along Spark's neck she could feel a silent growl rumbling through her fingertips. A mixture of anxiousness and hope tightened in her chest.

Could this be the lead they were looking for to find the drug runners who'd stolen the puppies?

But then to her surprise Asher barked out a laugh and shook his head as if he couldn't believe what he was hearing.

"You want me to take my boat across to Canada, grab a package and bring it back, and you won't even tell me who you are?" Asher asked. "All for a hundred bucks? You think I'm stupid? Thanks, but no thanks."

She blinked. What did Asher think he was doing? Was he really going to insult their only lead and send them away? Asher signaled Spark. Peyton dropped the leash and the dog ran to his side. Asher turned and walked toward the boat.

"You coming, baby?" Asher asked her.

"Fine, whatever!" the large man said, before she could answer. He swore. "My name's Vaughan." He nodded to his skinnier partner. "You can call him Ridges. I've got no clue who's going to be in the inflatable boat, and I can't budge on the hundred bucks. I'm just doing a favor for a friend and I'd do it myself, but I've got somewhere else I need to be—"

"Don't need to know all the details," Asher cut him off and held up a hand. "Your business is yours. Just wanted to know who I was dealing with." He nodded from Vaughan to Ridges. "It's all good. Tell your buddy I'll drop off his package in a bit."

He turned, started up the ramp and boarded *The Mixed Blessing*, with Spark by his side. Then he glanced back to Peyton and hesitated. It looked like he was mentally kicking himself for not waiting for her to board first. She smiled at him reassuringly and then, without a word, picked up the tray of coffees. She walked past Vaughan and Ridges, handed Asher the tray, and then untied the boat. Asher set the tray down and she tossed Asher the ropes. *The Mixed Blessing* began to drift away from the dock. She ran up the gangplank, Asher grabbing her hand and helping her on board. Then he pulled the gangplank up. They made their way to the cockpit and Asher took the wheel. The boat pulled out into the Salish Sea, headed for the Canadian border.

Silence fell, except for the gentle roar of the twin motors and the sound of water sloshing against *The Mixed Blessing*'s hull. Wind brushed her face and sent the ends of her blond wig dancing. It was only then she realized she was holding her breath and exhaled.

"What was that all about?" Peyton asked. "We get our first solid lead and you sounded like you were trying to pick a fight with our suspects? Were you really going to walk away from the deal if they didn't tell you their names? You know they could've been lying."

"Didn't want to look too eager," he said.

Asher's green eyes looked out over the water.

"Oh," Peyton said. She hadn't considered that. "Because they'll think you're a cop?"

"Partially," Asher said. "But more because I didn't want to look like this was my first rodeo. My dad was in sales and used to take me when he visited clients. One of his favorite tricks was to pretend he was willing to walk away. Gotta figure that any drug runner large enough to steal and hide three puppies for this long, while moving them around between locations, has to have a pretty lucrative operation."

"Spark definitely detected a smell on them," Peyton said. "But that doesn't mean they're actually carrying drugs right now. K-9s are trained to detect the smell itself, which can linger, sometimes for hours or even days after the drugs themselves are gone."

Like the smell of a barbecue hung in the air long after the burgers were eaten. The shore grew farther and farther behind them. Asher blew out a long breath, and she watched as a genuine smile crossed his handsome face. He looked relieved.

"Wherever you find a lot of dirty money you'll find a lot of criminals wanting their piece of it," Asher went on. "My guess is he'll have more drug runners than he needs and there might even be infighting between them. The fact we're not kids, have our own boat and that we've got one Canadian and one American on our boat, makes us a pretty tempting team. So, if I want him to trust me, I've got to show I'm willing to do the job but that I'm not a fool."

He ran his hand over the back of his neck.

"To be honest," he added, "I'm not sure I like how easy that was. We've been here less than twenty-four hours and we've already got someone wanting us to run drugs for them?"

He lapsed back into silence. Peyton stood beside him a long moment. Then she went and sat on the deck beside Spark. Towering rocks and majestic trees rose high around them on both sides of the straight. To their left lay the deep and endless waters of the Pacific Ocean. To their right was an intricate maze of islands and inlets that made up Washington State's north shore, and beyond that North Cascades National Park, where Asher and Spark had found the clue that had led them here. The beauty surrounding her was breathtaking.

"I got a whole bunch of different pastries," Asher said, "because I wasn't sure what you'd like."

"Thank you," she said. "I usually have yogurt and fruit for breakfast, but it'll be nice to change things up."

She wasn't used to letting somebody else take charge. As the PNK9's head trainer, she ran the kennels and was responsible for training all of the dogs that came through. She also traveled around Washington State to do field training with both the PNK9's dogs and those of other units. But working with K-9 officers was different than following somebody else's lead. Especially when the lives of those three missing puppies could hang in the balance. If she was honest, she wasn't sure what to make of Asher's plan. He seemed to think the best way to find the bloodhounds was to make sure they never tipped anyone off to the fact they were even looking for them. After all, someone had put an awful lot of hard work and trouble into keeping them from being found.

"We find the drug runner," Peyton said to herself, repeating the words Asher had said when they'd started the mission, "and let the drug runner lead us to the puppies."

It wasn't that she didn't trust Asher. She trusted him implicitly. Respected and admired

him too. He was an incredible officer, talented
and strong. While she'd never been a fan of
beards, she had to admit his undercover look
hadn't done a thing to diminish how handsome
he was and made his green eyes seem brighter
than ever. Tricky thing was that she'd always
had a bit of a crush on him too, despite the
fact Asher had a reputation for being a bit of
a grump and was open about the fact he was
committed to a bachelor life and didn't see
marriage in his future.

Or maybe she was attracted to him because
he was unattainable?

She'd never been one to make things easy
on herself and had pushed herself to work long
hours and take on challenging training above
and beyond what her job required. This assignment might be a good opportunity for her to
put the foolish crush behind her. It was easy
to idealize a handsome colleague from afar.
It was another thing entirely to have to work
closely with him in a high-pressure situation.
And just one day in, she'd learned he was the
kind of person who had a clear sense of what
was right and didn't take much time to consider other opinions.

The Canadian coast grew closer. Asher had
taken a meandering route, exploring the inlets
and coves, looking to anyone who might be

watching that they were indeed tour operators checking out the area. On the surface, the
rules for crossing into Canada by boat seemed
pretty relaxed. All Asher had to do was report
they'd arrived at Canadian Border Services in
person or by phone. Which made smuggling
look easy. The hard part was avoiding being
detected by the Shiprider Law Enforcement
Team, a vigilant unit comprised of both Canadian RCMP and American Coast Guard members who worked together to spot, stop and
apprehend traffickers. Chief Fanelli had coor-
dinated with the head of Shiprider about Asher
and Peyton's mission, and agreed to keep them
in the loop and pass on any intel they found.
In return, the Shipriders would conveniently
avoid searching Asher and Peyton for the du-
ration of the mission.

As Asher and Peyton neared the coordinates Vaughan had given them, Spark began
to growl. The dog stood and braced his paws
against the deck, as his tail swished. Under the
right conditions, a K-9 dog could detect scents
for miles away, and Spark had the additional
specialized skill of being able to detect objects
underwater. Peyton moved back to join Asher
at the wheel, as did Spark.

Moments later they saw the gray inflatable
boat skimming across the water. The small

boat had seemingly come from nowhere. Although she couldn't prove it, the odd thought crossed Peyton's mind that the boat might've actually come from American water.

The boat drew closer until it pulled up alongside *The Mixed Blessing*. The young man standing at the motor was shrouded in an oversize hoodie and didn't look older than eighteen.

"You Dan?" the kid called.

"Yeah," Asher called back. "And who are you?"

The kid didn't answer. Instead he pulled a brown envelope out of the inside of his jacket. It had been folded over double and was sealed with something bulky inside. His boat bumped against theirs. The kid stretched out his arm as Peyton leaned over the boat toward him, and the moment she had the package in her grasp, he gunned the engine and disappeared again.

Peyton looked down at the package. There was something printed on it in black marker.

"Gunther's Scuba Shop, Rock River," she read out loud. She looked up at Asher. "That's not far from where we were docked when those two guys approached us. Who's Gunther?"

"I have no idea," he said. "His name didn't show up on my background research. Although it's possible he's just a patsy, and the package is intended for someone else. Let's get back into American waters, call Jasmin and see what she can pull up on them."

If there was anything interesting to be found about Gunther and his scuba shop, the PNK9's tech expert, Jasmin Eastwood, would find it. This time Asher cut straight across the waters, taking the fastest possible route toward the American shore. Spark sniffed the parcel absentmindedly, then wandered toward the bow of the boat, curled up in a ball and closed his eyes. Peyton blinked. She turned to Asher. "Whatever this is, I don't think it's drugs."

His eyes widened. "Are you sure?"

"Spark didn't alert," she said. "And I trust Spark's detection skills better than any drug detection test."

"So do I."

Then what was she holding if it wasn't drugs?

"Should we open it?" she asked.

Asher frowned and his brows knit.

"It's a bad idea," he said. "If they think we've tampered with the package they won't trust us. Then again, I was counting on Spark to let us know what was inside." He looked toward the opposing shore. "I'm guessing you don't have a cell phone signal?"

She glanced at her phone and shook her head.

"Okay," he said. "Once we get back to the

American shore, let's find a quiet spot and then we'll see what's in the package."

*The Mixed Blessing* moved smoothly through the water until they reached the opposing shore. They pulled into a small cove outside of Salt Creek and dropped anchor.

Spark barked suddenly and urgently. A motor roared to the right. It sounded small and aggressive. She turned to see a figure clad in a wet suit speed around the corner standing on a Jet Ski. Goggles covered his face.

The figure raised his arm. There was a gun in his hand.

He aimed it at them and opened fire.

# TWO

She heard Asher shout for Spark to take cover. Then she felt his strong arms wrap around her. He pulled her down to the deck and sheltered her with his body. Gunfire exploded in the air above them. Bullets clanged against the side of the boat and ricocheted off the railing. Her heart pounded in her chest. She could hear prayers pouring from Asher's lips and joined in with her own pleas to God for help. The shooting stopped. She felt Asher pull away and realized he was going for his gun.

"Find shelter!" he yelled.

She crawled across the deck toward the companionway, reached the steps that led down into the small cabin below, crouched up on one knee and reached for her weapon. Although, as a trainer, she wasn't authorized to carry a service weapon, she did have her own small personal handgun tucked safely in her ankle holster. But she'd never aimed, let alone fired it, at another person before.

Their attacker stood on his Jet Ski just a few yards away. He'd stopped firing and seemed to be fiddling with his weapon. Had it jammed? There were black and smudgy lines on his wrist, in the gap of pale skin between the cuff of his wet suit and his glove. It looked like some kind of tattoo.

She heard the sound of loud and cheerful music floating across the water toward them. A civilian party boat was coming.

Worry stabbed her heart.

*Lord, please keep them safe. Please don't let any innocent people get hurt.*

She watched as Asher set the man on the Jet Ski in his sights. Then the figure with the tattoo turned around suddenly, sending a large spray of water flying out behind him as he took off down the shore. *Thank You, God.*

Peyton holstered her weapon and stood slowly on shaky legs. Asher summoned Spark and in an instant the dog was by his side. Then Asher's eyes met hers.

"You okay?" he asked.

"Yeah." She nodded.

She watched as he whispered a prayer of thanksgiving under his breath. Only then did he holster his weapon too.

The music grew louder, then seconds later a midsize yacht came into view. Half a dozen adults and almost twice as many kids crowded around the deck, bedecked in colorful rain jackets and windbreakers to protect against the drizzly weather. A brightly colored plastic banner flapped from the sail wishing Tommy a Happy Tenth Birthday. She blew out a long breath. The situation could've gotten so much worse.

"Text the chief," Asher said, "and report this. Tell him we'll call as soon as we're docked somewhere safe."

She did so. Asher raised his now empty hands and waved at the yacht.

"Ahoy, there!" he called. "Happy birthday!"

The children and a few of the adults waved back.

"Everything okay?" a middle-aged man at the wheel called. He'd cut the engine but the boat kept slowly drifting past. Concern creased his face. "We thought we heard some kind of a bang?"

The man mimed a finger gun out of the children's line of sight, as if to ask Asher and Peyton if they'd heard a gun.

"Some idiot on a Jet Ski set off some kind of explosive device," Asher called back. His voice was confident and reassuring. His head shook like he was wondering what the world was coming to. As Peyton watched, the other man relaxed. "My wife's just calling it in to the authorities now. But I don't think you folks need to worry about it. Although it's always good to stick to popular routes. You never know what kind of nonsense people get up to when they think nobody's around. You guys have a good day!"

"You too!" the man called back.

The children waved again and the boat continued its slow journey down the shoreline.

"My guess is that whoever just fired at us didn't want an audience," Asher said, "so they took off when they heard that boat coming."

"Did you notice the gunman had a wrist tattoo?" Peyton asked.

Asher's eyes widened. "No."

"All I could see was a swoosh and a line," she said. "It seemed pretty rough. It could've been a fish, a vine or a geometric shape for all I know."

"Would you recognize it if you saw it again?" Asher asked.

"On someone's wrist, probably," she said. "Not sure if I would if I just saw a picture of it on the wall at a tattoo parlor."

Asher nodded and watched as the party boat grew smaller on the horizon.

"I suggest we follow them at a distance," Asher said, "head back to Rock River and call Chief Fanelli from there."

Peyton nodded.

"I just texted him what happened," she said, "and to expect our call. Also, to ask Jasmin what she could find out about Gunther's Scuba Shop, Ridges and Vaughan."

"Speaking of which," Asher said, "I think it would be a good idea for us to look inside the package and see what somebody just shot at us over."

He pulled the package out of his jacket and called his K-9 partner. Spark dutifully trotted over, sniffed the package and didn't signal. Then Spark glanced up at Asher and his shaggy eyebrows rose as if to say there was still nothing there.

"Okay, buddy," Asher said and ran his hand over the back of the dog's head. "Thanks for double-checking for me."

Then Asher rubbed his beard. It wasn't the first time she'd noticed him do that and she figured he was still getting used to having it.

"Well," he said, "I'd rather open the envelope and then have to talk myself out of whatever mess that might get me into with the drug runner, than not open it and discover I delivered something worse than drugs into the hands of criminals."

She stood by his side as he slid on a pair of gloves, then slowly peeled the adhesive back and gingerly reached in. He pulled out a baggie and held it up for her to see.

A few dozen loose cigarettes lay inside. That's all? Asher blew out a hard breath.

"Gotta say I did not expect that," he said. He turned the envelope this way and that, shook it a little, then opened it and smelled the inside. "I'm no K-9 but these definitely look like ordinary cigarettes to me."

Her mind boggled.

"Well, that would explain why Spark didn't detect anything," she said. "He was never trained to detect tobacco. There's definitely a major problem with black market cigarette smuggling in this area. Is it possible that whatever Vaughan and Ridges are involved with has nothing to do with drugs?"

Or the stolen puppies? Was their first solid lead a dud?

"Everything about this is fishy," Asher said. "I feel like we're being tested. But I don't know who by or why. How much do you think this baggie of cigarettes would be worth on the black market?"

"I don't know," she said. "Maybe twenty or thirty bucks?"

"That's what I'd say too," Asher said. "So it's kind of strange Vaughan said our cut would be a hundred. But I don't see anything else hidden in the package."

They made their way back to the Rock River marina. Asher eased *The Mixed Blessing* back into their rented slip and moored it. Then they checked the hull for signs of damage, thankfully finding no more than a dent and a couple of scratches in the yellow paint from where the tattooed man's bullets had struck. The man on the Jet Ski may have been gutsy, desperate or both, but thankfully his aim hadn't been that great. Asher's words earlier about how criminals had no shortage of people willing to do their dirty work crossed her mind.

Was the man who shot at them a big fish or a small fish? And how did Vaughan, Ridges and Gunther's Scuba Shop fit into all this? Either way it seemed like someone wasn't happy that Asher and Peyton had moved in on their turf.

There were enough people and boats moving around the marina, she didn't think the tattooed man would make another attempt on their lives. But no one was close enough that they had to worry about being overheard.

Peyton sat down in the bow cross-legged. As

Asher sat down beside her, she handed him an earbud and put the other one in her ear. Spark ambled over and curled up at their feet. She held the phone up between them so that she and Asher could both look at the screen.

Chief Donovan Fanelli's face appeared. The head of the PNK9 unit was a tall man with graying brown hair. He was sitting at his desk at headquarters in Olympia, his aging K-9 Malinois, Sarge, beside him. Worry filled the chief's eyes.

Asher quickly filled their boss in on everything that had happened so far, from dropping hints that he was interested in taking on some illegal side jobs, to Vaughan and Ridges approaching them, to the pickup, the gunman with the tattoo and then finally discovering what was in the package.

"I'm glad to see you're both okay," Donovan said. "How are you two now?"

Asher glanced at Peyton. "I'd say we're both irritated and worried, but no worse for wear. There's some slight cosmetic damage to the boat but nothing that will seem suspicious."

Donovan nodded.

"We've made both local police and the Shipriders cross-border patrol aware of the situation," Donovan said, "and Jasmin's been looking into Gunther's Scuba Shop."

The chief turned the camera so that they could see the PNK9's tech expert, Jasmin, sitting at one of his guest chairs, her laptop and phone in front of her. She raised a hand and waved.

"I also looked into the thugs Vaughan and Ridges," Jasmin said. "Unfortunately, I don't have enough to find a match yet. On the other hand, I can tell you that Gunther Feret moved to the United States from Germany six years ago. He opened a gym in San Diego. Three years ago, he met his wife, Annika, in a body-building competition. Gunther quit competing and they moved up here and opened the scuba shop."

"Any criminal record?" Peyton asked.

"Gunther has a few speeding tickets," Jasmin said. "Annika once took out a restraining order against an ex-husband. But nothing in either of their pasts that would spark suspicion."

"How about suspicious properties?" Asher asked.

"Just the store and a house in the woods," Jasmin said. "No other properties registered in their names."

"Why did Gunther quit competing?" Peyton asked. "Any significant injuries or incidents?"

"Not that I've found so far," Jasmin said.

"Good question though," Asher said. "If so,

it could explain a need for extra money or an addiction to drugs himself."

He sounded impressed, and Peyton felt a flush of heat rise to her cheeks.

"Any employees?" Peyton asked.

"Annika has an adult son named Finn from her previous marriage who briefly helped around the shop a few months ago," Jasmin said. "He's twenty-three. Rumor is there's no love lost between him and Gunther. It seems like he hasn't been around for months and there's no one else. It's a family business."

Peyton thought about the package they were supposed to deliver to the shop—seemingly just cigarettes. "So, it's possible that Gunther's Scuba Shop has nothing to do with this," she said.

Jasmin and Donovan nodded.

"Could be," Jasmin said.

Asher sighed and ran his hand over his beard.

"Well, there's only one way to find out."

They ended the call with the promise they'd touch base again later when Asher and Peyton were back at their suite in the lodge. Then Asher, Peyton and Spark walked down the marina and through Rock River to Gunther's Scuba Shop.

It was about a twenty-minute walk. The small store sat on a picturesque main street that had colorful brick stores lining one side, with a boardwalk, railing and benches overlooking the water on the other. At first glance the stores all seemed to be joined together like townhouses, but as Asher grew closer he could see that some had narrow alleyways cutting between them, which he expected led to a larger laneway out back. The scuba shop had a big picture window, filled with large multicolored hanging fish and an entire family of mannequins in scuba gear. Its brick exterior was painted a bright and cheerful shade of green.

"Looks like the kind of place somebody really cares about," Peyton said softly.

"Yeah," Asher said. Not what he'd have pictured as a hotbed of criminal activity, but drug fronts came in all shapes and sizes. He gestured to a bench in front of the window. "Wait here. I won't be long. I wish I could leave Spark with you for backup, but I need his nose. I want to see if he alerts to anything."

Peyton's eyebrows rose. "You want me to wait outside?" she asked. "Why?"

"I don't know what we're going to face in there when I try to deliver this package," he said, "and it's safer for you to stay outside."

*Because you were already shot at once today, and I can't focus on the mission if I'm worried about protecting you.*

He watched as she bristled, and for a long moment he thought she was going to argue with him. If she had, maybe he'd have even backed down. But instead all she said was, "Okay, you stay safe."

She turned and walked to the bench. As he watched, she opened her cell phone's web browser and started researching local tattoo parlors. He turned and walked into the store.

It was well-kept and empty except for a short man behind the counter with very muscular shoulders and hair so blond it was almost white. Asher pretended to wander for a moment, as he cast a quick glance around to make sure the store was empty and give Spark a moment to sniff around. The dog didn't alert.

"No dogs allowed in the store," the blond man said without looking up.

Asher ignored the comment, summoned his inner Dan Johnson, walked over to the counter and leaned against it.

"You Gunther?" Asher asked.

The man grunted. "I am."

Gunther cast a dirty look toward Spark, but before he could repeat what he'd said about dogs not being allowed, Asher pulled the package out from the inside of his jacket and laid it on the counter.

"Some friends of yours asked me to drop this off to you," Asher said.

Gunther's face didn't move a muscle. The man opened the bag, dumped the baggie out on the counter and glanced at it. Asher had the impression he was counting the cigarettes. Then Gunther shrugged and pushed the entire thing back across the counter toward Asher.

"I don't know what this is," Gunther said. "You must have the wrong place." Gunther pointed to a No Smoking sign by the door for extra emphasis. It was next to a rack of all organic healthy supplements. "Get this garbage out of here."

Frustration rose to the back of Asher's neck. He'd just risked Peyton's life, Spark's life and his own all to get a baggie of loose cigarettes for this man who was now telling him they were worthless. He swallowed hard, pushing the anger down into his gut, and prayed for patience. Up to this moment part of him had secretly been hoping there was something valuable hidden in this bag after all. Maybe the fact Gunther really did think it was useless was a clue in itself. Although for the life of him, Asher couldn't see right now what that would be. He had to focus.

How would Dan Johnson be feeling right now? How would he react?

Asher glanced quickly over his shoulder to make sure someone hadn't walked in without him noticing. When he confirmed they were still alone, he leaned across the counter and pulled off his sunglasses so that Gunther could see the emotion in his eyes.

"Is this some kind of joke?" Asher hissed. "If so, it's not very funny. My wife and I arrived here in town last night, with our dog, planning to stick around for a bit to build up our tourism boat business. I may have mentioned to a few people I wasn't opposed to a bit of side work if anyone needed help transporting anything across the Salish Sea to Canada. These two guys, calling themselves Vaughan and Ridges, show up at my boat and start cutting eyes at my wife."

He searched Gunther's face for a reaction to the men's names, but Gunther shrugged impassively as if the story bored him.

"They ask me to do you a favor by picking something up for you," he went on. "So I did, because I'm a nice guy and I figure it never hurts to make friends with local businesses." He strategically decided to leave out the whole matter of the hundred dollars. "Now we're on our way back and some idiot on a Jet Ski starts taking potshots at my boat. Chipped my paint, dented my hull, and scared my poor wife and dog to death."

Gunther's eyebrows flickered up, but only a fraction of an inch, and within a second his placid face returned. Asher paused and swallowed a breath as if he was fighting the urge to swear or punch a wall but thought better of it and caught himself.

"I don't know about you," Asher said. "But I don't like being made a fool of."

He paused a long moment, letting uncomfortable silence fill the small shop.

"And I don't like it when people try to mess with me or my business," Gunther said. A steel edge ran through his voice. "Did you call the police?"

"Would you?" Asher asked, rhetorically. Then he pulled out one of his fake business cards and slapped it on the counter. "Do me a favor. If you think of anything about why someone would've done this to me—to us— give me a call. I'd rather deal with it myself without getting police involved. And if you ever need help, and aren't messing around, you know where to find me."

Asher hesitated, waiting to see if Gunther would reach for the package. When the other man didn't, Asher scooped it up and stuffed it in his jacket. Then he turned and walked out of the shop.

"Sorry, somebody wasted your time," Gunther called after him. "If I can ever help you out with some scuba gear let me know. I'll set some aside for you in case you ever want to dive. It's a pretty popular activity around these parts."

Asher waved a noncommittal hand over his shoulder.

He stepped outside into the misty air and took a deep breath.

What had that all been about?

Then he turned to the bench where he'd left Peyton. His heart stopped. She was gone.

# THREE

Peyton slipped down the narrow alleyway between two stores and followed the sound of shouting. Moments earlier she'd been sitting on the bench, trying to watch through the large store window as Asher had been having what seemed to be a heated discussion with the man behind the counter, only to notice Vaughan and Ridges coming down the street toward her. Her heart had started racing, trying to strategize what her Merry Johnson identity would say to them, when they'd turned down a narrow alley between a coffee shop and a clothing store before they reached Gunther's. They didn't even seem to see her there. Then she heard the sound of their angry voices rise. It sounded like the two thugs were fighting about some major deal that had gone wrong. She'd prayed and then followed, in the hopes of overhearing something that would explain what was going on, knowing it might be her only opportunity to figure out what these two men were really after.

The narrow space between the two stores was only a few feet wide and empty except for overflowing garbage and recycling bins. It branched off into two directions at the end, and she could hear the sound of yelling echoing from somewhere just out of sight.

By the sound of things, Vaughan was verbally tearing into Ridges for losing over a hundred thousand dollars' worth of "merchandise." He was furious and frustrated, and his shouts seemed to amplify as they bounced off the brick walls around them. And Ridges, the smaller of the two, wasn't mustering much she could catch in terms of his defense.

"I don't want excuses!" Vaughan snapped. "I want you to go back out there and find the merchandise. I put my neck out on the line for you. You'd be dead if I hadn't defended you to the boss. You think you can lose multiple assets like that and just walk away?"

What assets had Ridges lost? Her heart stopped. Was it the puppies?

The average purebred bloodhound puppy cost a little over twelve hundred dollars. While stealing and selling one would be a good way to make some quick money, the fact that whoever had nabbed them had apparently kept them this

long and moved them from location to location
meant the criminal had something else in store
for them. It didn't make sense. Puppies were
more valuable for sale than older dogs. And
Rottweilers, boxers and German shepherds all
seemed like a more obvious breed of dog for
a criminal to want for security or protection.
Chief, Agent and Ranger had been adorable
puppies, with their tan and black markings,
long silky ears and big dark eyes. They'd been
incredibly intelligent too and excelled in their
K-9 training. But none of that explained why
cross-border, drug-running criminals would
go to so much trouble to move them around
and keep them hidden for this long.

What did they want with her precious pups?

She couldn't make out what Ridges mumbled
in reply, only the angry shout that Vaughan
shot back in response. "Nobody loses or steals
merchandise and lives to talk about it!"

Peyton pressed her back against the painted
brick. Her heart pounded so hard in her chest
she could barely breathe. The baggie of loose
cigarettes might have been a test to determine
if she and Asher were trustworthy enough to
join their criminal organization. Or a diver-
sion to get "the Johnsons" out of the way, shot
by the tattooed man to eliminate any potential competition. Either way it was clear that

whatever Vaughan and Ridges were involved with, it was much bigger than cigarettes and something the boss was willing to kill over.

The voices were moving away from her now as Vaughan and Ridges strode deeper into the labyrinth of back alleys that ran between and behind the stores. She followed at a safe distance and crept forward one silent step at a time. She couldn't back down, not while she was so close to finding out more about their operation.

If she'd walked away, and it then turned out that they had stolen the puppies and gotten away with it, she'd have never forgiven herself.

"How could you be so stupid!" Vaughan bellowed. "Now you're going to die, and I'm probably going to get murdered right alongside you, unless we find them and fast!"

"They're in a cave—" Ridges yelled.

"Yeah, but what cave?" Vaughan cut him off. "Where is this cave? You don't know! You can't find it!"

Peyton reached the end of the alley and risked a quick glance around the corner. It was only for a fraction of a second before she pulled back out of sight again. But it had been long enough to see both men wielded guns. Vaughan was waving his around in the air in all directions at once, like it was a conductor's baton, directing his own orchestra of anger and profanity. But Ridges had his weapon clamped in his arm, down by his side, in a white-knuckle grip.

"It's not my fault, okay!" Desperation rose in Ridges's voice. "I didn't pack nothing! I didn't choose using water bottles!"

Water bottles? The words echoed through Peyton's mind.

So, this wasn't about the puppies?

Something clattered behind her. Peyton turned and looked to see a cat—calico and sleek—scamper out from behind an overturned garbage can and take off down the alley.

"Who's there?" Vaughan shouted. She heard their footsteps pounding down the pavement toward her. "You come out now, with your hands up, or I'm going to put a bullet through your brain."

Peyton turned and ran.

Desperately, Asher's eyes scanned the boardwalk. His hand tightened on Spark's leash, and he found himself fighting the urge to call out Peyton's name.

Where was she? Where had she gone?

Barely five minutes had passed since he stepped out of the scuba shop and found her missing. But already he could feel worry clogging his chest, tightening his lungs and making it harder to breathe.

*Help me, Lord, I need to find her. Please let her be safe.*

Then he saw Peyton, sprinting out from between two stores ahead of him. He ran for her, and her eyes met his. They were wide and filled with terror.

"What happened?" he asked. "Are you okay?"

But her words tumbled over his in a rush to come out.

"I was eavesdropping," she said. "A stray cat blew my cover." Who? Why? Where? He didn't know and for now it didn't matter. Asher could hear the sound of people running down the alley toward them and angry voices shouting. "I need to hide before they find out it was me."

Asher reacted without thinking. He dropped Spark's leash. Then he swept Peyton up into his arms, spun her around and turned them both toward the metal railing overlooking the water. He stood with his eyes facing the Salish Sea and Peyton's back pressed up against his chest. Then he pulled her closer to him so that anyone glancing quickly wouldn't even notice her there tucked inside the shelter of his arms. Strands from her blond wig caught the wind and tickled his face. He signaled Spark to his side and the dog lay down at his feet.

"Relax," he whispered to Peyton. "I have an alibi. I was in Gunther's shop."

"But I don't," Peyton said.

"Yeah," he said, "but guys like that won't see you as a person or as a threat, just as my woman."

An odd strangled gasp slid from Peyton's throat, and he wondered if he'd said something wrong. He heard the sound of Vaughan and Ridges stomping down the boardwalk behind them.

"Where'd he go?" Vaughan shouted.

He? So they'd apparently assumed whoever had been eavesdropping on them had been a man.

"How should I know?" Ridges shot back.

Asher felt Peyton stiffen in his arms.

"Just relax," he whispered. "Deep breaths in and out. We're just like any other couple relaxing and looking out at the water. They probably won't even notice us here, and if they do, I'll cover for you, and I've got Gunther as an alibi."

She leaned back and he felt her cheek brush against his bearded jaw. It didn't escape his attention that they'd been together on this mission less than twenty-four hours and he'd already found his arms wrapped around her twice. Three times if he included when the gunman had opened fire.

"How did things go with Gunther?" she asked.

"Badly."

Questions swirled through his mind. Peyton had been eavesdropping on Vaughan and Ridges? How had she found them? What had they said? What had she overheard? He could hear the two thugs disappear down the boardwalk still on the hunt for whoever had been eavesdropping on them. He forced his own breath to slow and silently counted back from a hundred in his head. Then, he finally pulled away from her and slid one arm around her shoulders.

"Come on," he whispered in her ear. "Let's walk back to the boat and fill each other in. Seems we both have a lot to talk about."

He looped Spark's leash around his hand. The three of them strolled back down the boardwalk toward the marina. He forced himself to walk slowly as if he didn't have a care in the world. But they'd hardly gone a hundred steps when he saw Vaughan and Ridges storming back along the boardwalk toward them. It was clear that they were angry and searching for someone.

Vaughan looked at Asher. His eyes narrowed.

*You're not Officer Asher Gilmore of the PNK9*, he reminded himself. *You're Dan*

*Johnson. You smuggle drugs, and you just got played.*

"One moment," he said and handed Peyton Spark's leash.

Then he strode down the boardwalk toward the men.

"Hey!" he shouted. He yanked the packet out from inside his jacket and waved it at them. "What was this about, eh?"

He stopped walking a few feet ahead of them. They stopped walking too. Then Asher hurled the package at them with such force it hit Vaughan's arm, bounced off and landed on the ground by their feet. He waited to see how they'd react. Would they grab it? Or ignore it like Gunther had? Ridges glanced at it but didn't reach for it. Vaughan didn't even look.

Huh, interesting.

"Am I some kind of joke to you?" Asher demanded. "I do you guys a favor and end up getting played?" His hand jabbed through the air like a blade. He pointed from them back toward Gunther's store. "You want to tell me what all this is about?"

Vaughan stared Asher down as if he'd already wanted to take a swing at somebody else and Asher happened to be the wrong guy in the wrong place at the wrong time. The large man's hands balled into fists, and Asher suddenly realized that if he didn't back down, Vaughan might actually hit him.

Only he couldn't imagine Dan Johnson backing down, even if it meant getting slugged.

*Lord, help me find a wise way out of this.*

Then he felt Peyton's gentle hand take his.

"Come on, honey," Peyton said. "Let's keep walking." Her voice was so light, sweet and caring it almost trilled. He couldn't help but notice how natural the term of endearment sounded coming from her lips, while every time he'd tried to do something similar it felt like he was trying to speak some foreign language he didn't understand. Peyton scooped the package up off the ground and handed it to him. "This isn't worth fighting over. Let alone getting yourself into trouble about. Just take some deep breaths before you do something you'll regret."

To his surprise, Asher found himself being led away down the boardwalk by his imaginary wife. He tucked the package back inside his jacket.

Then Peyton glanced back over her shoulder and called, "Sorry, fellas, my guy gets a bit hot under the collar sometimes. Let's all just clear this up later when everybody's calmed down."

He waited until they'd walked a safe distance away from the men and then leaned toward Peyton.

"I can't believe you just apologized to them," he whispered.

"Oh, I didn't apologize to them," she said. "Merry Johnson did. She knows her new husband can be a bit short-tempered and does her best to keep him out of trouble."

"I like it," he said. "You're really good at this."

He glanced at her. A hint of a smile crossed her face. It was beautiful.

"Now, why did you throw our only clue at him?" she asked.

She sounded genuinely curious, not accusatory, and he realized she trusted him.

"Gunther wasn't interested in the package," he said. "The fact the men who sent me after it don't care about it either pretty much proves that the package itself is worthless, and that whatever reason they had for sending us on the wild-goose chase isn't about the contents. I thought it was possible that there was something else hidden in the package, or the cigarettes themselves, that we didn't see."

"Like diamonds or state secrets?" she asked.

He snorted. "Exactly, like diamonds. Or maybe the coordinates to some real drug runner drop-off."

No, this errand had been all about testing them, distracting them or getting them shot. Whatever the reason, they weren't going to get away with it. He quickly filled her in on what happened with Gunther, and she told him what she'd overheard Vaughan and Ridges saying.

Now to figure out what any of that even meant and plot their next step.

It seemed clear that some major drug operation had gone wrong, over a hundered thousand dollars of merchandise had gone missing and they were now in some caves Ridges couldn't find.

Huh. Asher wondered what all of that meant to their case.

They made it back to *The Mixed Blessing*. While he knew they'd have both liked to go to their suite at Stark Lodge and regroup right away, it was more important they keep up their cover story. So they sailed around the Olympic National Park coast, Olympic Peninsula and Strait of Juan de Fuca, stopping in at small marinas and chatting to the locals about the sights.

The coast included seventy-three miles of breathtaking wilderness, rain forest and beaches. Olympic Coast National Marine Sanctuary was home to over a hundred and fifty historical shipwrecks, one which dated back to

1875. Multiple people told them that the local scuba diving was extraordinary and several recommended Gunther's as the best place to rent equipment.

Whether they liked it or not, it seemed "Dan" might have to take up Gunther on his equipment rental offer.

Even though Spark's keen nose worked overtime investigating each area they visited, he didn't alert once. The sun was dipping low below the horizon when Asher, Peyton and Spark finally returned to the Stark Lodge close to Olympic National Park. For Asher, there was something bittersweet about the fact they'd chosen a suite there as the home base for their undercover mission.

The lodge was one of three that had been owned by Stacey Stark, who'd been murdered along with her boyfriend, Jonas Digby, in Mount Rainier National Park several months ago. Asher's half sister, Mara, had dated Jonas until he broke up with her for Stacey. Mara had been seen fleeing from the murder scene— by PNK9 officers. A witness even claimed to have seen her *shooting* the couple. And Mara remained on the run.

While Asher was absolutely convinced, beyond a shadow of a doubt, that Mara couldn't have committed these crimes, officially the

PNK9 weren't weighing in on Mara's innocence or guilt, which had caused some tensions between Asher and other members of the team. But now, finally, there was a new suspect: Stacey's former business partner, Eli Ballard, who ran the three lodges. Until recently, Asher's colleague Ruby Orton had even been in a romantic relationship with Ballard. That was how off their radar he'd been as a potential suspect. Not only did Eli have a solid alibi, he'd been helpful in the investigation, and was always polite and friendly to the officers when they had questions.

But when evidence had come in linking Eli to a threat made against the Gilmore siblings' father, the team had quietly reinvestigated the lodge owner. Mara had been largely uncommunicative during the months she'd been in hiding, but she'd sent Asher a text referring to his and their father's life depending on her staying in the shadows. The team had had no idea what that could mean. Until a man matching Eli's description had been seen taking a picture of Asher and Mara's father from afar by staff at the care home where their father, who had dementia, lived. Why else would Eli Ballard have been there, taking a photo, if he wasn't connected to the murders—and to possibly frame Mara Gilmore for the crimes?

The team was working on the loose threads. Everything was being looked at twice.

Asher's last phone call and text exchange with his half sister had been challenging. Mara wanted Asher to protect their father—who Asher hadn't spoken to in years—while Asher wanted Mara to stop running, turn herself in and trust him to take care of her. She'd apparently decided she was better off on her own.

Before booking the suite for the undercover mission, Jasmin had confirmed that Eli had recently taken a leave of absence from running the lodge and had put an acting operations manager in charge. So it was unlikely that Asher or Peyton would spot him while there. But that didn't stop Asher from hoping they'd uncover something at the lodge that would help clear his half sister's name and bring her home. Just in case, they would be in disguise whenever they were out of their rooms.

Peyton led the way as they walked down the lodge's ground floor hallway back to their suite. They'd chosen a room at the very end of the hall beside the emergency exit so it would be easier to come and go without being noticed. As she reached for her key card, he could feel Spark's tension down the leash. He glanced down. The dog's tail swished. His K-9 partner sensed drugs. But where? Peyton tapped the key card to the door handle. The light didn't flash green, but when she touched the door-knob it began to swing open under her touch.

Suddenly Spark barked a sharp warning. Then the dog began to growl. His hackles rose.

Was there someone there? Had someone broken into their room?

# FOUR

Asher watched as Peyton froze. The door had opened a few inches. Her hand was still on the door handle and his partner, Spark, was growling up a storm. Peyton's eyes met Asher's.

"I only trained Spark in drug and underwater detection," she whispered. "He shouldn't react this way to anything else."

Asher's jaw clenched.

"Well, I doubt our hotel suite has found itself underwater," he whispered back, in a bad attempt at easing the tension building at the back of his neck. When they'd moved in, he'd checked the position of the closest hallway security camera. Was it working? Did it have a blind spot? Had someone broken in another way? "But maybe one of our friendly neighborhood drug dealers let themselves into our suite and is waiting on the other side of the door to have a chat with us."

"Maybe," she said. "Or they planted drugs in our suite."

Nah, he didn't think so. His mind immediately jumped to much worse scenarios. With his right hand, he pulled his gun from his ankle holster. With the left, he reached for the door handle and grasped it, brushing Peyton back and positioning himself between her and the suite.

"Stay behind me," he said.

He dropped the handle and kicked the door. It flew open, and the suite's living room came into view.

It had been tossed. The pillows from the pull-out couch were strewn about with the zippers pulled back as if somebody had been searching inside them. Every drawer of the TV unit was open, and the books, maps and Bible that Peyton had set out to give the room a lived-in feel were scattered across the floor. Their empty suitcases and outdoor gear had been yanked from the closet and the bedroom door on the left was closed. But wind whipped through the wide-open glass sliding door that led out to the thick forest beyond. Silence fell, punctuated only by the sound of tree branches shaking and Spark's low and relentless growl.

Frustration burned inside him, along with a deep sense of dread that tasted like ash in his mouth. He'd failed at their mission. Their cover had already been blown. It had to have been. He hadn't told anyone he'd talked to over the course of the day what town they were staying in, let alone the specific lodge or the room. So, what other reason could there be for someone breaking in and tossing their room? Maybe they'd traced Dan and Merry. Maybe they were tied to the murders Mara was accused of and had realized who Asher was. Either way, the operation had barely begun and it was already over.

The only question that remained for Asher was whether the intruder had escaped through the patio door or if they were still lying in wait. Asher steadied his weapon and turned toward the closed bedroom door. His voice rose to alert whoever might be lurking behind it.

"This is the—" he started instinctively.

But before another word could cross his lips he felt Peyton's hand grasp his arm and squeeze it so hard he almost winced.

"Oh, Danny, honey!" she cried. "I think we've been robbed!"

She'd cut him off. He glanced toward her and watched as a stern warning filled her hazel eyes, as if she knew she'd stopped him before he could say, *This is Officer Asher Gilmore of the Pacific Northwest K-9 Unit.*

Peyton didn't think the operation was over and wasn't about to let him blow it.

How could she be so hopeful? Someone had clearly found out where they were staying and broken into their suite. She pushed the door closed and then leaned toward him.

"We can't give up hope on finding those puppies," she whispered softly. "Not yet. They need us."

"Okay." He pulled away from her grasp.

He'd do it her way. Nothing wrong with hoping for the best, while preparing for the worst.

"Yes, sweetie," he said loudly, and the word felt as odd on his tongue as "baby" had. "I can't believe something like this could happen. I'm going to head straight down to the front desk and give them a piece of my mind!"

He crossed through the living room and closed and locked the patio door. Then, silently, he gestured to the bedroom door and held up his hand to signal Peyton to stay put. She opened her mouth as if she was about to say something. Then she closed it again and nodded.

As he signaled Spark to his side, the dog obediently joined him, but Asher sensed his partner was reluctant to leave Peyton.

He pressed himself against the doorframe and nudged the bedroom door with his foot.

It swung open. The bedroom was empty, but it was clear someone had been rummaging through it. Drawers were open, clothes were strewn across the floor and the mattress had been partially pulled off the bed.

It had been agreed, after some pushback from Peyton, that he'd be the one to take the pull-out couch in the living room and she'd sleep in the bedroom. When they'd checked in, Peyton had diligently set up the suite to look like a happy couple was staying there, unpacking Dan's and Merry's clothes in the dresser and laying their toothbrushes side by side on the counter, so that no one in housekeeping would think Dan wasn't sharing a room with his wife. At the time he'd wondered if her attention to detail was a bit of overkill. Now he was thankful she had done it.

But they'd locked their personal cell phones, wallets, IDs and laptops in the bedroom closet safe. He peered inside the closet expecting to find it open and the safe empty.

The safe was still locked. He punched in the combination and opened the door. All of their stuff was still there. He breathed out a sigh of relief and prayed.

*Thank You, God.*

"Safe was still closed and everything in it

is still here," he called and heard Peyton echo his prayer thanking God.

He closed the safe again. Asher couldn't believe how utterly convinced he was of the very worst and how quick his mind had been to jump there. When he'd seen the room, he'd been positive their cover had been blown. Had he always been this pessimistic and cynical?

*Thank You for Peyton too. I'm so glad she was there and stopped me from announcing myself as a police officer.*

Spark was growling again, though with that low rumble in the back of his throat that told Asher something was wrong. Had Peyton been right and someone had planted drugs in their room?

Then Spark barked a sharp and sudden warning.

And he heard Peyton scream.

Asher burst back into the living room. His heart stopped. Peyton stood frozen in fear. A man in dark clothes, a ski mask and swim goggles stood behind her. He had one gloved hand clamped over her mouth. The other held a knife to her throat.

Spark's barking rose to a protective snarl. Peyton's hazel eyes met his. Fear and fierce determination battled in their depths. Then she glanced to the hallway door and back as if silently signaling that's where her attacker had come from. Had he been lurking in an adjacent room or behind the emergency exit door? Had Spark detected the lingering scent of drugs on him, and was that why his K-9 partner been so reluctant to leave Peyton's side? Then her gaze darted to the gloved hand that clenched over her mouth. What was she trying to tell him?

Asher raised his gun with two hands and set the invader in his sights.

"Let her go," he ordered. "Now. Or I won't hesitate to shoot you."

The masked man didn't answer. Instead, he inched toward the sliding glass door, holding Peyton in front of him like a human shield. Asher aimed at the man's temple. It would be a tightened, tricky shot, but one which he had no doubt he'd be able to make to save Peyton's life.

"This is your only warning!" Asher's voice rose. "Let her go and get down on the ground! Now!"

Even as he said the words he could see Peyton's eyes begging him not to take the shot and he knew why. If he killed this man there'd be no way to explain to the likes of Vaughan and Ridges why he'd miraculously escaped jail bars. Dan Johnson would no longer be some cocky nobody and a prime candidate for a bit of light smuggling because he wasn't on the police's radar. Their undercover operation would be over, along with any hope of finding Chief, Agent and Ranger.

*But I'm sorry, Peyton,* he thought, hoping she could read his thoughts in his gaze. *If I'm forced to choose between finding the bloodhounds and saving your life, I'm picking you.*

Spark barked wildly. Asher took a deep breath and steadied himself. Peyton closed her eyes and took a deep breath, mirroring his. As she did, the silent attacker's knife inched away from her throat.

Peyton's eyes snapped open. She attacked, raising her elbow high and knocking the knife away from her neck. Then she wrenched her head away from the man's grasp and bit his hand so hard he yelped in pain.

The masked man shoved Peyton toward Asher so hard that she flew across the room. Asher dropped a hand off the gun and caught her in one arm to break her fall. Her attacker ran for the sliding glass door, yanked back the lock, flung it open and dashed out into the trees.

Asher glanced at Peyton. "Are you okay?"

She steadied herself and gasped a breath.

"I'm fine," she said. "It's the shooter. He has the same tattoo!"

The man who'd shot at them from the Jet Ski had somehow found their room, ransacked it and grabbed Peyton?

"Are you sure?"

"Yes!" she said. "Go!"

Asher signaled Spark to his side and ran for the door.

"He's not a pro!" Peyton called after him. "He's an amateur! He doesn't know how to restrain a hostage and thought the knife would scare me into submission."

Well, clearly he had another think coming.

Asher ran down along the side of the lodge, in the narrow gap between the wall and the tree line. He could see the man ahead of him. The figure was running in a zigzag motion, ducking behind trees and around patio furniture, as if he knew exactly where the security cameras were and how to dodge them. Asher pressed on.

He wasn't Officer Gilmore anymore on his way to arrest a suspect.

He was Dan Johnson.

A man whose hotel suite had been broken into.

A husband whose wife had been manhandled and threatened.

Someone who was out to do business on the wrong side of the law.

He'd catch this guy, pin him down and get answers. He might even let him go and tail him or have a colleague in the PNK9 arrest him. Either way, Asher was getting answers.

The walls branched out toward the woods. The perp dove deeper into the trees and then disappeared around the side of the lodge. It was clear wherever this man was going he knew the lodge's layout well.

Asher may have lost sight of him, but Spark's keen nose wouldn't let them down. Asher and his partner rounded the corner—right into a tall fence that hemmed in the recreational area. A storage shed lay directly in front of his nose, blocking the section of fence from view. Spark barked at the fence and then spun in a circle as if as frustrated by the barrier as Asher was.

"I know, buddy," Asher said. "We've got to find a way to get you around to the other side."

They ran down the side of the fence. Asher spotted a gate and pushed through. The sound of cheerful voices and happy children rose to greet them. Asher holstered his weapon and stepped farther in, with Spark at his side. A large pool with a children's play area, three hot tubs and a partially covered snack bar lay to their right, along with several doors leading back into the lodge. Manicured lawns dotted with hedges, tables and chairs lay to their left.

A few families had braved the waters of the heated pool despite the chill in the October air. Adults cluttered around the bar and patio area. Asher heard the sound of a car peeling out of a parking lot somewhere out of view.

He led Spark back down the fence to the place where they'd lost sight of the masked attacker.

"Find him," Asher told his dog softly.

The dog sniffed the fence, caught a scent and followed it to the storage shed. His black-and-white ears perked and Asher followed him across the lawn toward the pool. Then Spark's confident gait slowed, and he whimpered and shook his head from side to side.

Spark took a few steps toward a group of adult women who were enjoying drinks in the hot tub. Then he paused as if second-guessing himself, woofed under his breath and started toward what seemed to be an open utility door where a small cluster of male staff were smoking what Asher could guess at a glance weren't all cigarettes, only to stop again and turn toward the bar area.

The canine had been trained to detect drugs—not to chase individual people—and right now it seemed his excellent nose was confounded by multiple scents.

"It's okay, buddy," Asher said softly. "Just do the best you can."

But even as he watched his partner continue to sniff the air he could tell it was no use.

The man who'd attacked Peyton was gone.

Peyton wasn't sure how long she stood there in the shambles of the hotel suite as she tried to calm her racing heart. While she might've gone through the same training as K-9 officers, there was a world of difference between a training exercise and having an actual criminal holding a knife to her throat. And while she'd managed to keep her wits about her when the attacker had suddenly barged through the door behind her, now her legs shook so hard it felt like they were about to collapse beneath her.

Then a distant memory of something her late grandfather used to say flickered at the edge of her mind—when you don't feel strong enough to stand, there's no shame in kneeling before your Creator.

She double-checked that the hallway door was closed. Then she knelt down beside the pull-out couch, closed her eyes and prayed.

*Dear Lord, thank You for getting me through today safely. Thank You that Asher was there to shield me from the shooter on the water and to help me escape him just minutes ago. Please help Asher and Spark catch him. Help us find the puppies. And help me to serve You and seek justice to the best of my ability today and every day. Amen.*

"Housekeeping!" A cheerful female voice sounded along with a rapping on the suite door.

Peyton opened her eyes and looked up. A young woman, who looked barely twenty, with a pear-shaped figure and shoulder-length curls, stood in the doorway in a crisp uniform pushing a housekeeping cart. Her smile was wide, but as she looked at Peyton it faded and concern washed over her features.

"Oh, I'm sorry," she said. "The door just opened when I touched it. Are you okay? Are you hurt? Do you need help?"

She rushed across the floor toward Peyton and reached out her hands as if to help her up. Her name tag read Ember.

"I'm fine," Peyton said quickly and stood. "I think something's wrong with the locking mechanism on the door, because I just tried to lock it."

But when she, Asher and Spark had arrived at the suite the sliding door had also been open. Had someone broken through the main door and then opened the sliding door? Or did he come in through the sliding door and then jimmy the hallway door so he could come back later?

"I am so sorry about all of this," Ember said,

looking around at the mess in the suite. "What do you need? How can I help?"

The young maid's care and concern was so genuine Peyton felt it touch something inside her. Especially when she considered Ember's own employer had been murdered earlier that year. While Peyton hadn't been involved in the investigation into the murder of Stacey Stark, who'd owned this lodge and two others, she knew that both Stacey's business partner, Eli Ballard, and Asher's missing half sister, Mara, were considered suspects. But she'd never really stopped to think about the lives of the people who worked at the lodges and how the situation would've impacted them. Had Ember known Stacey? How had life been for lodge employees as the investigation dragged on?

Peyton took a quick breath and tried to think of what Merry Johnson would say.

"I'm okay, really." She curled her lip in a grimace she hoped landed somewhere between frustration and irritation. "My husband and I got back from doing some sightseeing and walked in to find some joker trying to rob our room."

She'd decided to stick as close to the truth as possible while undercover. Peyton searched Ember's eyes as they widened and saw nothing there but genuine worry.

"We actually saw the guy run out," she added. "My husband and dog chased after him."

Peyton debated mentioning being attacked by the masked man then decided not to disclose that until she'd talked with Asher. Instead, she silently prayed Asher would catch him without blowing their cover.

Ember reached into the pocket of her uniform and pulled out her phone.

"We need to call the police," she said, "and let the manager know."

"I've already reported it to law enforcement," Peyton said quickly, which again, was technically true considering Asher and Spark were K-9 officers.

She reached out her hand to touch Ember's arm and breathed a sigh of relief when Ember stopped dialing.

Now what? Merry and Dan Johnson's room being tossed had been seen by housekeeping. Police had to get involved, somehow, otherwise it would raise even more questions.

"Thank you for your help," Peyton said and meant it. "I really appreciate it. My husband and I are really private people, and we'd prefer nobody makes a big deal about this. Would you mind heading down and letting the manager know in person? And asking him to keep it quiet?"

Ember's worried eyes glanced around the room for one more moment as if debating whether it was safe to leave Peyton alone. Then she said, "Okay, and when I get back I can help you tidy up a bit."

"Thanks," Peyton said. "But I want to go through everything personally to see if anything has been stolen."

Especially since she still didn't know who the man with the wrist tattoo was, why he was targeting them, and what he might've seen or stolen.

Ember started out the door. Then suddenly she stopped, turned back and glanced down the hallway in both directions as if making sure no one was listening.

"The temporary manager, Mr. Skerritt, is going to tell you that nothing like this has ever happened before," Ember said in a hushed tone. "It's not true. There've been a lot of thefts. But nobody ever presses charges and somehow the lodge always gets away with sweeping it under the rug."

Peyton felt her eyes widen.

"Have they all been like this?" Peyton asked.

"No." Ember shook her head. "It's all been small stuff. People saying someone rifled through their suitcase and drawers."

Whoever was behind this could be escalating. But did it have anything to do with the stolen puppies? Or the double murder?

Ember disappeared down the hallway. Peyton prayed God would help them solve both crimes, whether they were connected or not. Then she locked the door again. This time Peyton was extra careful to make sure the door lock was turned all the way, and even though it seemed to work she noticed it didn't fully click into place.

Asher and Spark still weren't back, so she got her work cell phone from the safe, stood by the sliding door to keep an eye out for them and called Chief Donovan Fanelli.

"Hello, Peyton!" Within moments the chief's commanding and comforting voice sounded down the phone. "I wasn't expecting to talk to you until later. Everything okay?"

Peyton quickly filled him in on everything that had happened and the wreckage their suite was in now.

"He was wearing a ski mask and leather gloves," she added, "so I don't think we're gonna get much in terms of DNA or fingerprints. The most important thing to me is maintaining our cover and not blowing this operation. I don't think we can get away with not calling the police, but I also really don't think Dan and Merry are going to want law enforcement poking around their business."

"Agreed," Donovan said. He blew out a breath. "I'll send Jackson. He and Rex are at the PNK9 training center right now. Shouldn't take them too long."

Excellent choice, Peyton thought. As a K-9 team, Officer Jackson Dean and his protection Doberman, Rex, had an intimidating air about them, coupled with genuine and tender hearts of pure gold.

"I'll put a call in to local law enforcement letting them know this is part of our ongoing operations so that they don't send their own guys if the lodge calls them," he added. "Also, I'll send Parker Walsh with Jackson as well. Our four candidates for the two open slots on the team will be wrapping up their time with us soon, and I'd like for you and Asher to assess Parker while he's helping out. I'll be having the other three candidates assist you and Asher on this operation on various things behind the scenes."

For months now, the four candidates had been working with the unit. Each was a fully trained K-9 officer who wanted to join the highly esteemed PNK9 team: Parker Walsh, Veronica Eastwood—who was their tech expert's sister—Owen Hannington and Brandie Weller. The plan had been for them to shadow the PNK9 on cases as a try-out period, and at the end the chief would choose two of them for a permanent position on the team. Rumor was that one of the candidates—Parker—was trying to sabotage the others' chances of getting hired. But was there any truth to that?

There had supposedly been some dangerous incidents over the past few months but with little proof of who was behind it all. Working out of the training center, Peyton wasn't always fully in the loop. She just hoped Parker—the one who'd be coming to assist her and Asher—wasn't guilty of anything.

She thanked Donovan and ended the call. Moments later she saw Asher and Spark approaching from the back. She opened the sliding door for them. Asher's eyes met hers, he shook his head and she knew in a glance that the masked attacker had gotten away. Asher and Spark slipped through the door, and she locked it behind them. He quickly filled her in on how they'd lost the man with the wrist tattoo behind a storage shed in a busy area. She gave him a very brief rundown of her conversations with Ember and Donovan.

Asher ran his hand over his beard.

"Yeah, you're right that Dan is not going to like having the police here," he said. "But Jackson is a great call. We haven't always seen eye to eye on Mara's situation. He definitely wasn't about to jump to assume she's innocent, like I have. But he's kept an open mind, and he's a terrific cop."

Asher blew out a breath and ran his hand over the back of his neck. Peyton knew it couldn't have been easy to have his colleagues thinking his sister could be a murderer.

"Parker's got a reputation for being a very competent officer," Asher said. "But he's also rubbed a few people the wrong way. Owen, Veronica and Brandie have all faced some…" He paused again as if debating the best word to use. "Unfortunate challenges. Owen claims he got a weird text sending him on a wild-goose chase that could've jeopardized an active operation. Veronica said someone put her in a very bad position that delayed her from assisting on a case. Then this summer Brandie was pushed into traffic."

"That all sounds pretty serious," Peyton said.

"Yeah," Asher added. "Some people think Parker was sabotaging them to ensure he landed one of the permanent spots."

"What do you think?" Peyton asked.

He frowned. "I don't know what to think. Parker has come across as a bit arrogant and maybe he has bragged about his accomplishments—*and* he's been around for all those incidents. But that doesn't make him guilty."

Given that his own half sister looked guilty of the crimes she was suspected of committing when Asher believed she was innocent, Peyton wasn't surprised that he wouldn't judge Parker without solid evidence.

A flurry of knocking sounded on the suite door. Asher told Spark to stay with Peyton. Then she could practically see Asher slipping into his Dan persona as he strode over to the door to answer it.

It was a tall man in a tan suit, who introduced himself as Acting Operations Manager Ray Skerritt. He was somewhere between his late thirties and early fifties, Peyton guessed, with a weak chin and the kind of bland features some people had probably considered handsome when he was younger. Ember and a handful of other uniformed housekeeping staff trailed behind him.

"I'm so incredibly sorry for all this," Ray said. "We take the safety and security of our guests very seriously. I can assure you nothing like this has ever happened before!"

Asher crossed his arms and scowled. His bulk filled the doorway, blocking the man from entering. She listened for a moment as the acting manager tried to talk Asher into letting him into the suite to see the mess for himself and Asher repeatedly refused, in a calm but frustrated tone that made it clear how completely unimpressed he was with the lodge, its security, Ray's babbling excuses and the man himself.

It sounded like Ray was offering to comp one night's stay and give them a free upgrade to the Honeymoon Suite. In the late spring, her friend Officer Willow Bates had stayed in the lodge's Presidential Suite with her then-estranged husband, Theo, while working a serial-bomber case. Peyton had specifically asked for that larger suite when she'd booked and been told it was unavailable. Now she was curious to see if it was the same suite and Ray was just giving it a different name to appease the newlyweds. Hopefully it wasn't some tacky pink-and-red suite with heart-shaped furniture.

While Asher kept Ray and the housekeeping staff at bay, she went into the bedroom, got their camera from the safe and started taking pictures of the mess, documenting it as best she could. Minutes later she heard Asher's voice rise in a frustrated roar as Jackson and Parker arrived. The men played their parts well. Jackson insisted loudly and calmly that he was an officer of the law and that Asher needed to let him in. Parker then cleverly added that the call had been placed by Merry and they had an obligation to ensure she was safe and well. Asher shot back that if either of them touched anything there'd be trouble to pay, and he wasn't against punching a man who messed with his wife or his dog, even if he did have a badge.

Then Jackson and Parker entered the suite, along with Jackson's Doberman partner, Rex, while Asher continued to stand at his post blocking the door. Peyton nodded to the two men, thankful to see a friendly face. Rex and Spark happily wagged their tails to each other in greeting, and Peyton was glad Asher had thought to leave Spark in the suite, so the dogs' friendship wouldn't give anything away.

They set to work, taking pictures of the mess, going through it with gloved hands, looking for any evidence they could find and having Spark sniff thoroughly for drugs. They analyzed the scene without talking so they wouldn't risk being overheard by anyone in the hallway, although she imagined Asher's angry bluster would be doing a pretty good job of drowning out their voices.

"Asher's really selling it hard, isn't he?" Parker whispered in a low voice, as he walked past Peyton in the kitchenette. "Guess he's finally putting that chip on his shoulder to good use."

Peyton felt her neck stiffen. Yes, she knew Asher had a reputation for being stubborn, especially where his sister, Mara, and father were concerned. But she wouldn't go so far as saying he had a chip. More like he was shouldering a much heavier burden than people realized.

As she suspected, the search didn't turn up anything, and as Jackson and Parker wrapped up, Peyton wondered if all they'd really accomplished was bolstering her and Asher's cover. If word did get back to Vaughan, Ridges and whomever they were working for about the break-in at the suite, she suspected Asher's angry defiance that he didn't want cops poking around in his business would help solidify his reputation. Asher might even be able to swing this whole incident to his benefit. Jackson offered to stick around a bit to help Peyton and Asher pack and tidy up. But while she appreciated the offer, they all knew there was no way a lingering police presence would help their undercover operation.

Jackson and Parker thanked her, nodded to Ray and left. Asher shoulder-checked Jackson hard as he passed in the hallway outside the door. Jackson swung back and his right hand balled into a fist as if the two men were on the verge of coming to blows.

Instead, Jackson pulled back, said, "Watch yourself!" and left.

And Peyton had to quickly cover her face with her hand to keep from smiling at the men's impressive and improvised theatrics.

Asher told the acting operations manager to give them some time to pack up and came back into their suite. Then he pushed a table in front of the door to keep out any more unexpected visitors. She leaned over it, glanced through the peephole and waited until the hotel staff was gone. Then she turned to Asher. He was standing by the couch with Spark by his side and his face still set in a scowl, like he was still wearing his "Dan Johnson" mask.

"I've pretty much finished packing up," she said. "You'll want to go through your stuff and make sure nothing's missing."

"Okay," he said. "I told them I'd call the front desk when I'm ready for them to come and show us to our new suite."

She hesitated a moment, wishing she knew the right thing to say to make Asher's Dan-face melt back into the wonderful, handsome smile that had brushed his mouth back on the boardwalk.

Instead she turned and headed into the bedroom. The sooner they packed up and moved, the sooner they'd be able to have a real conversation about everything that had happened today and their plans for the ongoing mission to find the missing pups.

She laid her suitcase on the bed, unzipped it, and packed her clothes, books, electronic devices and toiletries inside. Then, she remembered the spiral-ring notebook she'd used to create Merry's journal sitting in the bedside table. She pulled the drawer open. It was empty. She got down and looked under the bed. Then she stood up and scanned the room. She couldn't find it anywhere.

"Ash?" she called as she felt the color drain from her face.

"Yeah?" He popped his head around the doorway.

"I think the tattooed man stole Merry's diary."

# FIVE

"He stole your diary?" Asher asked. He crossed the floor, took her hand and led her to the farthest corner of the suite, as if he was worried someone might reappear in the hall and try to listen in at the still-broken door. "Why would you… I mean… I know you… There's no way you'd leave something out of the safe that could blow our cover."

She shook her head.

"Not my diary of the case," she said. "I wrote a fake diary for Merry about her feelings for Dan."

"But why?" His eyebrows rose. "Why would you go to all that work for something you had no reason to suspect anyone would see?"

"No, I wrote it for me." Peyton broke his gaze, looked down and was suddenly aware that he still hadn't let go of her hand. She hadn't pulled away either. "I wanted to try and get my head around how Merry would feel about Dan. So, I made up a story of them. Stuff like how they met, fell in love and got married. How Dan proposed. What their wedding was like. I decided their wedding was in the summer, but they couldn't take time off for a proper honeymoon because it was peak tourist season, so they were having their real honeymoon now."

Asher was still gazing at her like she was a puzzle he wanted to solve. She hadn't realized that the sun had set or the clouds had moved in again, but now she was suddenly aware of the gentle sound of rain pattering against the darkened windowpane. She never expected to tell anybody about the journal—especially Asher. They hadn't planned to go into any specific details about the relationship aspect of their cover story. And maybe it had been silly to fill page after page with romantic notions like that, spinning a fairy tale about how much Merry loved Dan and how excited she was to be married to him.

"I heard whenever a person's head is stuck on something, writing about it can help," she added.

"But why were you stuck on how Merry loved Dan?" he asked.

*Because I have a pretty big crush on you. But that's not very professional of me, is it?*

*So, I hoped this would help me separate the fake marriage we'd be living for this mission from the real relationship we'll never have.*

The words she knew she'd never say flew across her mind.

"You've been married before," she said, reaching for the second-best, but still honest, explanation she had. "I haven't. I just thought it would help me get my head in the game."

He stepped back and their hands fell apart.

"Trust me," he said. "The only thing I've learned about being married is it's not for me and I'm never going to do it again." Asher grimaced as if he had a bad taste in his mouth. "Just as long as there was nothing in it that could've compromised the mission."

"No, not at all," she said.

"Good." He turned and started gathering his clothes. "I'm guessing he stole the journal to give to Vaughan and Ridges, to figure out who we are and what they're dealing with."

"Maybe," she said. "Although it's possible he's not working with them. Also, Ember mentioned that there have been small robberies here at the lodge for months and people haven't wanted to make a big deal about it. Maybe our thief has been stealing people's journals and personal devices in order to blackmail them into not calling the police."

Asher paused and turned back. That quizzical look was back on his face again.

"You might be right," he said. "After all, you were right and I was wrong when I assumed our cover was blown. Thank you for that."

He turned back to packing before he could see the flush Peyton felt rise to her cheeks.

Minutes later Peyton, Asher and Spark were leaving their hotel suite, walking down the hallway and heading up to the second floor accompanied by Ray Skerritt, who was still babbling on about how much he appreciated their discretion and how dedicated Stark Lodge was to making it up to them. If all thefts had been minor and the lodge always went above and beyond when they were reported, that could also explain how they'd managed to go under the radar for so long. The suite was at the very end of the top floor down a long and private hallway. As they reached the room, she saw Ember leaving with her housekeeping cart. She smiled at the young woman as she passed and softly thanked her again for her help earlier. Ember smiled back.

Despite her fears of being inundated with visions of pink and red hearts, the suite was rustic and every bit as homey and woodsy as the suite they'd left. It was much larger though, with a large crackling fireplace and a crescent-shaped couch that she could tell at a glance would fold out into a bed far larger and nicer than the pull-out Asher had in the smaller suite. There was a coffee table that seemed to have been crafted by a single large log and a sweeping balcony that spanned the entire suite.

She watched Asher's green eyes brighten as he took it all in. But he managed not to smile and to maintain his gruff composure as he briskly thanked the manager and saw him to the door. Asher locked it behind him and double-checked the dead bolt. This time the door lock stayed firm.

Then he turned to Peyton and held one finger to his lips to remind her to stay quiet. She nodded, and he pulled an electronics detection device from his pocket and carefully scanned every inch of the suite for video or recording devices, paying special attention to the ceiling vents and wooden chandelier. While she waited for him to finish, she silently summoned Spark to her side with simple hand gestures and commanded him to search too. Spark started sniffing.

Both searches turned up empty.

"All clear for me," Asher said and slid the device back into his pocket. He looked down at Spark. "All clear for you?"

Spark barked in confirmation and thumped his tail on the floor.

"Good job." Asher reached down and scratched the dog behind the ears. "All done."

Spark walked over to the fireplace and curled up on the rug in front of the fire. Peyton pulled her blond wig off carefully, unpinning it from the myriad of clips she had hidden underneath.

"I'm actually impressed you got him to follow nonverbal hand gestures only," Asher said. "I tend to rely on verbal commands."

"I always aim to triple-train all dogs in verbal commands, hand gestures and using a clicker," Peyton said. "Some dogs respond better to one than the others. I'm sorry, I probably should've double-checked with you before asking Spark to search, considering he's your partner."

"No worries," Asher said. He sat down at one end of the crescent-shaped couch and a slow grin crossed his face. "The way I see it, he was your pup before he was my partner."

She sat down on the opposite side of the couch and faced him.

"Recruit pups are like my kids," she said. And the newest three were still missing. And after a day of their undercover operation, they were no closer to finding them. "It's my job to train them and take care of them, before they head off to find their forever partners."

Was it her imagination or did his lips quirk slightly at the expression "forever partner"?

"Do you ever want to have your own?" he asked.

"Kids?" she asked. "I'd love to have a whole bunch of them. Four or five, even six. Not that I ever see it happening for me."

"Same," Asher said and chuckled. "On both counts. But I was actually wondering if you wanted a dog of your own. Or six."

She laughed.

"Yes, I'd like a dog or six as well," she said, "and a couple of cats. One day. For now my place is pretty small."

She felt a smile cross her face, and for a moment it was like she could see it echoed back at her through Asher's eyes. Then, just as quickly as it had appeared, she watched it fade again.

Asher pulled off the golden wedding ring he'd worn as part of their disguise and spun it around between his fingers.

"I'm sorry we haven't found the puppies yet," he said. "But I will do everything in my power to find them. I promise."

"I know," she said.

"I don't even know what to make of today," he said. "We were approached by Vaughan and

Ridges to collect a package from Canada that turned out to be nothing but cigarettes. We were fired at by a masked and tattooed stranger who also broke into our suite and threatened you. We were sent on some crazy errand to a random scuba shop. And now I've discovered that Stark Lodge has had a minor theft problem for months, which they've completely covered up. Which is maddening considering the PNK9 has been investigating Stacey Stark's murder for months."

"To be honest I don't know if I have a complete picture of that case," Peyton admitted. "I've never been fully briefed on it. I've only picked up things here or there. There've been so many times over the past few months I've wanted to ask you about it and see how you were doing, but I wasn't quite sure what to say."

His eyes met hers and held her stare. Something serious moved in his gaze.

"What have you heard?" he asked. "Be honest."

"About the case or about you?" she asked.

"Both."

She took a deep breath.

"In April, Stacey Stark and her boyfriend, Jonas Digby, were shot and killed near Logmire Suspension Bridge in Mount Rainier

National Park," Peyton said. "Mara was seen fleeing the scene, and she's been on the run ever since."

"And?" Asher asked.

"And she's obviously the prime suspect," Peyton said. "She used to date Jonas before he dumped her for Stacey. I heard you made it really clear to everyone who'll listen that you're convinced she's innocent. Forcefully."

"Forcefully, huh?" Asher asked. He leaned back and crossed his arms. "Did you hear I almost snapped at Jackson earlier in the summer during a team meeting when he questioned why she's on the run?"

"I heard you shot him an angry look," Peyton admitted.

"Well, he didn't deserve it," Asher said. He ran both hands through his hair. "Jackson is a fantastic officer, and he really saved our bacon by playing along so well with my little act back there. He was totally in his right to ask the question. I was just frustrated that I don't have a good answer."

"I also heard that Mara wanted you to check in on your dad," Peyton said, "and you were testy with some members of the team about that."

"That's fair," Asher said. "I talked to the staff at the care home where he was living and found out someone—who sounds exactly like Stacey's business partner, Eli Ballard—had taken a picture of him from afar. We moved my father into a safe house."

She'd also heard that he hadn't talked to his dad while he'd been at the home or afterward.

"Your father has dementia, right?" she asked. "I'm really sorry. My grandmother had dementia before she died, and there was something so incredibly exhausting about talking to her sometimes. She'd get so confused and I didn't know what to say. But I imagine it's different when you're estranged."

"My dad and I used to be really close when I was a kid," Asher said. "Or at least I thought we were. We did everything together. I was his little shadow. He used to take me on sales calls."

"What happened?" she asked.

"The official story is that he first cheated on my mom with a client of his when I was ten," Asher said. "Then after they divorced, he met Mara's mom, married her and they started a family together. That's what Mara, my mother and her mother believe."

"But you don't?" Peyton asked.

"I don't know what to believe," Asher said. "It all happened so suddenly, and my father always had a lot of female clients who he was really friendly with. Personally, I think that my father had multiple affairs. I also suspect that he and Mara's mother got involved before the divorce because of how quickly they got married. But I don't know for sure. My dad never wanted to talk about the past. And now that his memory is gone there's no way I'll ever know the truth."

"I'm sorry," she said. "I can't imagine how hard that must be."

It was the longest she'd ever heard Asher open up about himself and his life. Maybe the most anyone had recently. But while there was still much she wanted to ask him, a dark cloud had moved over his eyes and somehow she knew he wasn't ready. So she just sat there, carefully working free the remaining bobby pins that fastened her braided hair to her head and listening to the sound of the rain falling, the fire crackling and Spark's wheezing breath. And for a long moment neither of them said anything.

Asher glanced at his phone.

"Anyway, we've got half an hour before our meeting with Donovan," he said. "He just messaged me to fill me in pretty much on everything he told you, about having the four candidates on board to help us do some of the legwork on this case. We've definitely got a lot to fill him in on. I just hate to think we might've spent months spinning our wheels getting nowhere."

A knock sounded at the door. She leaped to her feet, tossed a throw pillow over her wig and then ran to the bathroom where she grabbed a towel and wrapped it around her head, careful to hide every wisp of red. When she came back Asher and Spark were on their feet. Asher pulled his weapon from his ankle holster.

"Check and see who it is," he said. "I'll cover you."

She walked to the door and looked out of the peephole to see Ember's cheerful face. She was standing at one end of what looked like a food service cart.

"It's Ember," Peyton said, "the housekeeper."

Asher tucked his weapon back into his ankle holster, pulled the cuff of his jeans down over it and then nodded to her. Peyton open the door.

"Ember," Peyton said. "It's nice to see you again."

"Mr. Skerritt wanted to send up a little something from the kitchen for your troubles," Ember said.

She wheeled the serving cart into the room, along with a thin young man around her age dressed in a crisp vest, white shirt and bow tie. His name tag read Laurence. Both of them wore plastic serving gloves. The cart was overflowing with platters and dome-covered serving dishes, but it wasn't until they started unloading the food onto the table in the living room suite that Peyton realized it was all for them. There were platters of fruit, veggie sticks, cold cuts and cheeses. There were baskets of bread and trays of pastries, cookies and cakes. Then they brought out two full steak and lobster meals, with all the fixings, and finally Laurence laid a bowl of what looked like homemade stew down on the floor in front of Spark.

Spark's ears rose to attention. He sniffed Laurence and for a moment Peyton thought he was about to signal. Then the dog shook his head, like he had water in his ears. Maybe somebody involved in the creation of the food had the scent of drugs on them or Laurence had but he'd showered it off. Either way, Spark sat and thumped his tail.

"The chef made it up special for him," Ember said. "We didn't have any dog food in the kitchen. So he made it from scratch. He says it's mostly beef with a bit of lamb and salmon mixed in, as well as sweet potato and carrots because his own dog is a fan of them."

"I'm sure it'll be fine," Asher said in a softer

version of his Dan-voice. "Definitely much better than the stuff he's used to having. Thank the chef for us."

Asher tipped them both. Peyton thanked them profusely, fighting the urge to hug Ember. Asher locked the door behind them and watched through the peephole. Then he whistled.

"Well, this is a lot," he said. "Not that I'm complaining. I wonder if they're worried that we called the police."

Spark sat patiently by his bowl and waited for Asher to give him the go-ahead to eat. Asher signaled that he could, and the dog chowed down happily.

"Spark definitely seemed suspicious of Laurence but didn't sense anything strong enough to signal," Peyton said.

"Yeah, I noticed that too," Asher said.

"As you know, some drugs can leave scents for days," she added, "like marijuana. Cocaine and methamphetamines are a lot easier to wash off. There might be an innocent explanation for Spark's suspicion."

"Or maybe not." Asher walked over to the table, picked up a frosted-glass bottle of mountain spring water and unscrewed the top. There was a metallic click as the seal broke. Suddenly a memory shot through Peyton's mind.

She'd overheard Ridges mention water bottles.

"Did you ever read that story about the Mexican smugglers who tried to hide knockoff painkillers inside glass pop bottles?" she asked.

Asher nodded.

"Cola and lime," he said. "Thought it would trick the drug-sniffing dogs at the border. Only border security insisted they open one and it all fizzed out like a soda geyser. I read about it when I was preparing to be partnered with Spark."

"Back in the alley behind Gunther's Scuba Shop," she said, "it sounded like Vaughan was furious at Ridges for losing drugs in some cave that were packed in water bottles. Ridges specifically said that water bottles float, so I'm guessing they're plastic not glass. What if whoever stole Chief, Agent and Ranger is trying to cross-train them to find those missing water bottles? The truck receipt clue which led us to Rock River was found in a cave in North Cascades National Park along with drug residue and bloodhound fur. If we can hone in on who might've packed these bottles, what happened to the missing ones and where they are now, we might be able to figure out who has our stolen puppies."

Ten minutes later, Asher was standing by the table, grabbing himself food and trying to pretend he wasn't fascinated by the way Peyton was setting up her laptop for the video call. First she'd moved to the middle of the crescent-shaped couch and opened her laptop up on the rustic wood coffee table. Then she'd gathered all the books and notebooks she could from around the suite and piled them up underneath her laptop, raising it higher and lower as she tried to find the exact right height.

He smiled. She'd finally unpinned her two braids and shaken her red hair loose so that it fell in long waves around her shoulders. She'd set each hair clip and pin in a glass ready for tomorrow. He suspected he could walk the floor barefoot in the pitch-black without ever having to worry about stepping on one. Peyton was so conscientious and detailed. He suspected nothing ever got past her. It was a good quality in a person. And a partner.

The call wasn't scheduled to start for a few minutes yet, but he guessed the message he watched her quickly type and send had been to Jasmin, because as Peyton opened the video chat, Jasmin's smiling face appeared on the screen. Peyton quickly filled the PNK9's tech expert in on everything she remembered Ridges and Vaughan saying in the alley and how she thought it might've been linked to what happened to the missing dogs.

A light shone in Jasmin's warm brown eyes. "I'm on it," Jasmin said, and the sound of her fingers typing filtered through the laptop speakers.

Asher turned back to the food. Odd that despite the incredible spread in front of him he still kept finding himself distracted by whatever Peyton was doing. The steak was so tender it pulled apart beneath his fingers. He slid a good-sized chunk of it between two pieces of bread from the basket and then added cheese from another platter for good measure. Then he started hunting around for some condiments to finish off his sandwich.

"I think I saw some mustard and another kind of dark-colored dipping sauce on the cold cuts platter," Peyton called. "And you can fish some lettuce and tomato from the salad."

He stopped and turned back. Heat rose to the back of his neck. Asher hadn't even realized that she'd been watching him too.

"Can I grab you anything?" he asked.

"Could you bring the veggie and cheese platters over?" she asked.

"You got it."

He balanced his makeshift sandwich on the corner of the veggie platter and carried them both over. Spark glanced their way from his usual post in front of the fireplace as if debating whether to join them, then stretched out slowly on the rug.

The laptop blooped and then Owen's face appeared on the screen. Tall, blond and having already made a name for himself on the force in Seattle, Owen, one of the four candidates, had the kind of clean-cut look that Asher expected to see beside the word "cop" in a kid's picture book.

Asher shuddered to think what someone would caption his own grumpy mug. Especially after the conversation he'd just been having with Peyton had reminded him of just how sour his mood had been the past few months.

"Hello, Mr. and Mrs. Asher!" Owen said. He grinned. "Wow, looks like they're feeding you well in the field!"

He chuckled. But Peyton's smile tightened as if something about Owen's comment had rubbed her the wrong way. Asher set the food on the table behind Peyton's laptop and then sat down beside her on the couch.

He leaned toward her. "You okay?" he asked, softly.

She nodded, sat up taller and straightened her spine.

Nah, she wasn't okay. But he didn't have time to ask her about it now.

The computer sounded two more times in

quick succession as first Donovan then PNK9 Officer Tanner Ford joined the call. Tanner wasn't the easiest guy to get to know—which Asher realized was pretty ironic coming from him—but he was tough, fearless and as solid as rock. By the look of things, Tanner was at home on his couch. His eyes seemed tired but focused, and his K-9 tracking boxer, Britta, lay beside him with her tan head on his knee. The final one to join was another one of the candidates, Veronica, who was also Jasmin's younger sister.

Donovan called the meeting to order and explained that Jackson, his K-9 partner and Parker were working on the investigation, and that Brandie, the other candidate, was doing some work for Jasmin. Then he gave a brief recap of everything that had happened in the case so far, including the fact Jackson and Parker hadn't found anything in their search of the suite.

"The fact a housekeeper says there have been ongoing thefts at the lodge for who knows how long and this is the first we're hearing of it really bugs me," Asher said. "It's possible that it means nothing and has absolutely nothing to do with Stacey's and Jonas's murders. It sounds like the other thefts were pretty minor and maybe the lodge talked the victims into sweeping it under the rug. But, it's a loose thread we're just discovering now and I don't like it."

Then Peyton filled them in on what she'd overheard Vaughan and Ridges saying about the bottles and their theory about how it might tie in with the dogs.

"I already think I've got something," Jasmin said. "End of May, Memorial Day weekend, a small foreign registered yacht set off Seattle-bound from Victoria, British Columbia. Canadian RCMP had gotten a tip there was a shipment of cocaine on board and the Shiprider Law Enforcement Team went to intercept. They boarded the boat and found nothing. But when they brought in the K-9 unit the dogs barked up a storm around an empty container of water bottles. They found one bottle, tested it and found cocaine residue."

Asher leaned forward. So did Peyton.

"That was about five months ago," Asher said. "The timeline works. So, what happened?"

"Well, the guy who'd rented the boat was a young Greek mucky-muck with diplomatic immunity," Jasmin said. "He claimed it was just a tourist trip he'd taken with his girlfriend, he'd never met the crew and when he caught one of the crew using cocaine he'd fired him on the spot, although law enforcement noted it looked like the unnamed crewman had actually popped off the boat and disappeared when they were docked in Port Angeles. The Greek consulate in Vancouver got involved and intervened. The mucky-muck and his girlfriend flew home. Not much law enforcement can do without evidence. Shiprider never got a proper crew manifest. Nothing there to chase. But theory was, someone had seen them coming and tossed the bottles overboard."

"Wow," Asher said. He looked at Peyton. "It fits."

"It sure does," she said. "Any idea how much cocaine is missing? The dollar amount?"

Jasmin's fingers tapped the keyboard.

"I'm only guessing here," she said. "But there are twenty-four bottles in a case—"

"And one was found empty," Owen added.

"Right," Jasmin said. "And I'm guessing at current street value each bottle would hold about fifty-five hundred dollars' worth of coke. So, fifty-five times twenty-three is a hundred and twenty-six thousand? Give or take a few ten thousand."

"Vaughan said that Ridges lost over a hundred thousand in merchandise," Peyton said. "It all fits."

Silence fell around the group as everyone took in the possible implications.

"Okay, so let's say someone on board the yacht saw Shiprider coming, thought fast and chucked all the bottles overboard," Asher said. "Maybe they panicked. Maybe they can't find them. Either way, now they're looking for them and have reason to believe they're somewhere off the coast of Olympic National Park. We cruised all up and down that coast today and the only time Spark alerted was in a cove near Salt Creek, right before we were attacked by the tattooed stranger."

"Maybe we should go back there tomorrow and give that area a closer look," Peyton said. "There might be caves."

"Agreed."

After some discussion it was decided that Asher and Peyton would rent scuba diving equipment from Gunther's in the morning and go search the Salt Creek cove. The chief suggested that they make arrangements for Spark to stay with Tanner and Britta during the dive, so that the dog wouldn't be left alone on *The Mixed Blessing* while Asher and Peyton were underwater.

"Sounds good," Asher said. "I don't exactly like the idea of leaving Spark alone on the boat, considering the last time we were there somebody shot at us."

"I'll take him and Britta hiking in Olympic Park," Tanner said.

"Thanks," Asher said. "He'll love that."

It was agreed Tanner would meet up with them in Rock River the next morning.

"I'll contact the Shiprider Law Enforcement Team personally to see what more I can find out about the yacht incident," the chief said. "There might be more than what's in the file, and I might be able to shake it loose. Owen and Veronica, I'd like you to get a sketch of the tattoo from Peyton and canvass tattoo parlors in Tacoma, Seattle, Port Angeles and the surrounding area to see if anyone recognizes it. Be discreet."

Was it her imagination or did Owen's smile dim slightly? She wondered if he was disappointed not to get a flashier assignment and if the fact that four candidates were being considered for only two spots was bringing out a competitive streak.

"Got it," Owen said.

"Absolutely," Veronica said.

"Okay," Donovan said. "Sounds good. Everybody stay safe and we'll meet up back here tomorrow afternoon to check in."

Asher and Peyton said their goodbyes, and the call ended.

Peyton closed the laptop, let out a long sigh

and walked over to the food table. He could tell at a glance her shoulders were tight.

"Everything okay?" he asked. "You seemed a bit bothered back there when Owen called you Mrs. Asher."

"I didn't realize you'd noticed that," Peyton said. "It's nothing personal. Believe me. It's just I worked really, really hard to reach the top of my game and prove myself, professionally. And suddenly it's like I've been demoted to your sidekick. 'The Mrs.,' 'sweetie,' 'baby.' You said it yourself, Vaughan and Ridges won't see me as a person, just *your* woman."

He knew she meant it when she'd told him not to take it personally. But still, something about her words stung in a way he couldn't explain. He stood.

"Well, just to be clear," he said. "I don't think of you that way. You impress me. Incredibly. You're talented and professional, and I'm incredibly thankful for how you had my back today. As for the fact I called you 'baby' or 'sweetie,' I'm still trying to figure out how Dan refers to Merry. But I'm sorry if I ever made you feel bad."

"No, it's okay," she said. A smile crossed her face that did nothing to assuage the look of sadness or worry in her eyes. "It's not you. I promise. I really enjoy working with you."

She made a plate of food then picked up her laptop and moved to one end of the couch. Peyton picked at her dinner as she sketched the lines of the tattoo on a piece of hotel paper. Then she showed it to Asher for confirmation, and when he nodded took a picture of it and sent it to Owen and Veronica. Then Asher and Peyton sat on opposite ends of the couch and worked on their laptops. After a while, curiosity got the better of him.

"What are you working on?" he asked.

"My schedule for the next few months," Peyton said. "Along with my job training at the center, I also travel around to do remote training in different areas and advise other K-9 units as my time permits. It gets pretty busy, and I like to have a good sense of what I'm doing to keep chaos at a minimum. So, I find it helps to plan it all out carefully in advance."

He thought about how she'd said she triple-trained each of her dogs in verbal commands, hand signals and clickers. Or the fact she'd gone the extra step of going through the K-9 officers' training program herself. He had so much respect for the work she did and how she approached it.

It was attractive. She was attractive, in so many ways.

But how could Asher ever get over his own

trust issues enough to build a real and lasting relationship with someone like Peyton? His ex-wife, Lucie, had an affair with a colleague on a business trip. He suspected his father had used his sales job to cheat with women behind his mother's back. While he knew Peyton would never use her work trips to do anything like that, he also knew it would be hard for him to get over his own trust issues to be with someone who had such a busy job. But he'd also never want someone like her to sacrifice any part of her career because of his own insecurities and mess. Maybe Lucie had been right, and he was the problem.

Asher took another bite of his steak, and even though his brain knew how delicious it was, somehow it tasted like sawdust in his mouth.

After a while, Peyton wrapped up the leftovers and put them in the suite's small fridge. Then she wished Asher and Spark good-night and went into the bedroom. He brushed his teeth, opened up the pull-out and lay there for a while listening to the sound of her keyboard clicking and clacking in the other room. Eventually the typing stopped, and he saw the light switch off from the crack underneath her door.

Asher closed his eyes and tried to sleep. But unwanted thoughts chased around his mind and wouldn't let him rest.

Finally, sometime after midnight he got up and slid his boots on. Spark's head rose instantly from the spot where it had been nestled in between his paws.

Asher signaled his K-9 partner to his side and clipped his leash on.

"Figure we both could use a walk," Asher whispered. At least he knew he could.

Asher grabbed the pad Peyton had used to sketch the tattoo and left her a note saying they'd gone for a walk, in case she woke up and found them missing.

Then he and Spark slipped out into the hallway. He locked the door behind them and checked it twice. Then he walked down a long and empty hallway to an access door, opened it to find a staircase and took it down to the main floor. It opened out into the trees. The rain had stopped, but the smell of damp earth filled his lungs. Silently they walked down along the back of the building in between the forest and the lodge.

Almost immediately Asher could feel his breath begin to slow and his heart begin to settle. He prayed and asked God to forgive his past mistakes, guide his future, help him find the missing puppies and bring Mara home safely.

He heard the sound of Spark sniffing the air.

He glanced down. The dog's ears were alert, his tail was still and his snout was raised as he smelled the night.

A warning shiver ran down Asher's spine. Spark sensed something.

A faint growl like distant thunder rumbled in the back of the dog's throat.

"Show me," Asher said.

# SIX

Asher and Spark moved swiftly down the side of the lodge, past the pool area and toward the parking lot, where he heard the sound of a voice shouting, a car door slamming and a vehicle peeling off into the night. He rounded the corner and almost collided headfirst with a diminutive figure, who was at least a good foot and a half shorter than he was. A female voice shrieked. Asher leaped back, pulled his phone from his pocket and switched its flashlight on.

Ember's terrified face blinked up at him in the light.

"I'm sorry," Asher said. He quickly lowered the light from her eyes. "I didn't mean to startle you. Spark and I were just out for a late-night walk and I thought I heard a ruckus."

He looked down at Spark. The dog's ears were completely relaxed now. Spark's head buffeted gently against Ember's leg as if reassuring her there was no reason to be scared.

Ember reached down and patted Spark's head and the dog's tail wagged. Whatever had been going on in the darkness outside the lodge in the middle of the night, this woman had Spark's seal of approval.

"What's going on?" Asher asked. "Is everything all right?"

"Everything's fine," Ember said, with a quiver in her voice that told him it was anything but.

"I heard shouting," Asher said.

Not to mention Spark had clearly sensed something was off and it didn't seem to be with Ember.

The housekeeper looked at the ground. "My boyfriend was mad I wouldn't cut work to go to a party with him. So, he lost it with me. It's not his fault. He was just upset."

Asher snorted.

"Well, that's utter nonsense," Asher said. "Any guy who tries to pressure a girl into going to a party with him after midnight and loses his temper when she won't is a two-cent punk who isn't worth your time."

He hadn't even stopped to think whether that was something Dan Johnson would say. Right now, Asher and his alter ego were on the exact same page.

"He's not a bad guy," Ember said unconvincingly.

All right, time for Dan to step up to the plate. Maybe with a little bit of Asher's truth mingled in.

"I don't know," he said. "Maybe he is. Maybe he's not. It's not my business. But I got a little sister around your age. She dated a guy, it turned messy and she got into some bad trouble. Really bad trouble. Look, Merry knows I'm not the perfect husband. But hopefully she also knows I really love her and respect her, and that I'm not just with her because she's pretty. Why are you even working this late, anyway?"

It had been hours since someone had broken into their suite.

"There's been some problems getting people to work shifts," she said. "We're short-staffed. People keep quitting. My boyfriend used to date another girl in housekeeping who quit a few weeks ago."

Sounded like the lodge had really gone downhill since Stacey was murdered.

"Heard a rumor somebody killed the owner a few months ago," Asher said. "Did that really happen?"

"Yeah," Ember said. She looked almost relieved that he'd changed the subject away from her boyfriend. "In April. We had two owners, Ms. Stark and Mr. Ballard. Somebody shot Ms.

Stark and her boyfriend. I heard it was his jealous ex-girlfriend."

That would be his half sister, Mara. Asher forced himself to let that slide.

"Things have been kind of weird around here ever since," Ember said. "Like there were a few minor robberies before she died, but it's gotten a lot worse."

"I take it people really liked Ms. Stark?" he asked. "More than Mr. Ballard?"

"No, not really," the housekeeper said. "Mr. Ballard is a real cutie. All the girls have a crush on him. But Ms. Stark was the one who made sure things got done."

Huh. Now that was interesting but not surprising.

"By the way, my wife Merry's been looking to get another puppy," he said. "One of the other guests said they heard some howling the other night. Does your boyfriend or any of his friends have dogs?"

Ember shook her head. "No, my parents have a couple of terriers, but they live in Portland."

Asher thanked her, waited until she was safely back into the building and then paused a long moment outside in the dark with Spark to make sure her unscrupulous boyfriend didn't show up to cause any more problems. Then he and Spark turned and walked back in the darkness toward the door that he'd come through.

His feet dragged with every step as if the accumulative burden of carrying all the questions that ran through his mind was weighing him down. He'd promised Peyton he'd help her find those bloodhound puppies and all he'd found was a housekeeper with a bad boyfriend, a string of unexplained thefts, a couple of drug dealers who'd sent him on a wild-goose chase to a scuba shop and a masked attacker who'd shot at them—and then held a knife to Peyton's throat.

The memory of that terrifying moment filled his mind.

Peyton had been in trouble, her life had been threatened and he hadn't been able to save her.

Something in his heart knew he couldn't let that happen again.

Peyton was standing on the deck of a boat. A storm was raging around her—waves crashed over the side, rain poured down around her and she could hear the bloodhound puppies howling and crying out for her. Agent, Chief and Ranger were scared. They needed her. But water streamed down her face, blinding her eyes, and she couldn't see them anywhere. She ran. Her feet slid on the slippery deck. The boat seemed to grow longer and longer beneath her feet. Suddenly the puppies loomed over her. Agent, Ranger and Chief were huge and monstrous now with snarling teeth and gigantic claws. She called their names and tried to signal them. But they'd forgotten who she was. She was no longer their trainer. She was their prey. Their jaws opened to swallow her whole...

Peyton sat bolt upright in the bed. Her heart pounded as fragments of her nightmare still flickered at the edges of her mind.

She'd spent months training Chief, Ranger and Agent. They'd been so sweet and intelligent. What if she was right in her hunch that whoever had stolen them was trying to train them to help their drug operation? Would they even recognize her if she found them again? What if her precious puppies were gone and there was no way to remind them of who they really were?

She closed her eyes and prayed.

*Lord, please let us find them before it's too late.*

She got up, dressed in simple jeans and a T-shirt and brushed her red hair down around her shoulders. Then carefully she combed the red hairs from her brush and flushed them down the toilet, so no one in housekeeping would spot any long red hairs. Silence fell from the other side of the door. She opened the door and stepped through into the living room of the suite.

There lay Asher, fast asleep on the pull-out couch, with Spark nestled beside him. The dog's furry head was tucked tightly into the crook of Asher's neck so that the man's chin rested just behind the dog's ears. Asher's left hand rested gently on the dog's side, and Peyton was suddenly aware that he hadn't ever put his pretend wedding ring back on since taking it off the night before—and that she'd forgotten to remove hers. She'd even slept with it on.

Peyton stood there for a long moment watching them sleep. A feeling she couldn't put into words swelled in her chest. If she'd hoped this undercover mission would help throw some cold water on her foolish crush on Asher, she'd been sorely mistaken.

And yet, how could she let herself develop feelings for a man who so clearly didn't want a relationship? Or relegate herself to being seen as someone's sidekick?

His green eyes opened, and a slow grin crossed his face. Then just as quickly as the smile had appeared it disappeared, and he sat up so suddenly Spark scrambled for a moment to resettle himself.

"What time is it?" he asked. "Is everything okay?"

"Everything's fine," Peyton said, "and it's ten to eight, which gives us a little over an hour before Gunther's Scuba Shop opens. There's a coffee maker, so I figured I'd make us some and we could have leftovers for breakfast."

Asher tossed the blankets off him and stood. He was still wearing the clothes he'd had on the night before. He'd even left his boots beside the couch. Spark climbed onto the floor and stretched, pressing his nose against the carpet and his tail up in the air.

"I took Spark for a walk around midnight," Asher said. "Spark alerted again. We ran into that housekeeper, Ember. She was clean, but she'd just had a fight with some bad-news boyfriend who'd just left for a party, so he might be who Spark detected. She told me the thefts got a lot worse after Stacey was killed. The lodge has been understaffed too."

"You questioned a suspect without me?" Peyton asked.

"You were asleep, and I just ran into her."

His tone was light. She knew he was right too, and she'd have done the same.

So why did it bother her?

Because maybe she was still a bit sensitive

about Owen's "Mrs. Asher" comment and being seen as someone's sidekick.

*Lord, help me sort my heart and keep it out of my mission.*

She went over to the curtains and pulled them back, sending the morning sun streaming into the room.

Asher inhaled sharply.

She turned back. "What?"

"Nothing," Asher said. He ran his hand over the back of his neck. Was it her imagination or was he actually blushing?

She crossed her arms and held his gaze. He looked away first.

"It's just your hair, okay?" he said. "It looked really nice and fiery all of a sudden when the sun hit it. You had it covered up under that wig all day, pretty much, yesterday."

Sudden electricity shot up her arms and heat rose to her face too. She walked past him toward the coffee maker, somehow not able to meet his gaze either.

"I thought gentlemen preferred blondes," she said.

"Maybe they do," he said, and his voice sounded a little bit lower and rougher than usual. "But I never claimed to be a gentleman."

She laughed and so did he. Then he slid his boots on, grabbed Spark's leash and took the dog for a walk, while she tried to tell herself that whatever had just happened between them was good-natured work banter and that they definitely hadn't been flirting.

By the time he got back, Peyton had already folded the sofa bed back into a couch, pinned her blond wig back over her hair and was sitting at one end of the couch with a fresh cup of coffee.

"I grabbed a couple of different flavors of yogurt from the restaurant on my way back," Asher said. "I remember you said they were your usual breakfast. Thought you might want to add them to the leftover fruit from last night."

He'd remembered.

"Thank you," she said. "That's really thoughtful."

Half an hour later they were back on board *The Mixed Blessing*. The lodge didn't have its own marina, but there was a marina only a short walk away in Puget Sound. Asher piloted the boat, while Peyton sat in the bow. She stretched her legs out in the sun. Spark lay beside her with his head resting gently on her knee. The weather forecast had warned them that rain would be returning with a vengeance later in the afternoon, but for now there were only a few wispy clouds at the edge of the horizon.

October in Olympic National Park was a time of transition and change. All around her she could see that the gentle green of maple, ash and aspen leaves had already begun to change into their vivid fall colors. By the end of October the entire forest would have transformed. During the summer, Olympic was one of the top five most visited national parks in the United States. But once the rainy season arrived in force by late October, the mass of tourists cleared out, and the park's rain forest came alive. Bright red, orange and yellow mosses coated the trees and colorful mushrooms sprung from the forest floors. The park would be pummeled by a good twelve feet of rain over the winter, while storms sent mighty swells and powerful winds to beat at the rugged shores.

*Lord, right now my heart feels like this national park around me. I'm caught between two seasons. Neither of which I fully understand. Part of my heart is longing for a relationship with a man like Asher. Part of me isn't ready to let go of the independence I have. Help me to trust You for whatever comes next.*

*And please, don't let my foolish heart threaten this mission.*

The Rock River marina was fuller than she'd expected it to be. Seemed the crush of tourists weren't quite ready to give up on the summer season yet. They docked at the same slip they'd had the day before, and then made their way to shore. Peyton and Asher both wore mirrored sunglasses and baseball hats, and Asher's ring was back on his finger. Asher held Spark's leash and walked so closely beside Peyton that their hands kept accidentally brushing against each other, sending confusing sparks flying up her arms.

It was incredible how easily Asher stepped into his Dan persona. The way he held his shoulders changed, as if he was intentionally making himself larger, and his jaw clenched as he smiled. He nodded to tourists, buskers and caricaturists as they passed, he handed out business cards to everyone they spoke to, and went out of his way to introduce himself to vendors and tell them about the business they were starting in the spring.

As they reached Gunther's Scuba Shop, Asher leaned toward her.

"I want the three of us to go in together this time," Asher said. "You're good at reading people, and it would be great to get your take on Gunther. I still have no clue what to make of our interaction yesterday." He grinned and his eyes twinkled. "Not to mention the fact you managed to get yourself into a little bit of trouble last time I left you out here unsupervised."

He was teasing her.

"Hey, don't forget I came back with a pretty big catch," she said.

He chuckled. "Like you'd ever let me forget."

She laughed so loudly that an elderly couple sitting on a bench by the water looked over at them and smiled.

"That's a beautiful wife you got there, son," the elderly man called with a twinkle in his eye. "You be sure to take good care of her, all right?"

"Yes, sir." Asher turned toward him and grinned broadly. "My wife, Merry, and I are opening a new boat tourist business in the new year. Got us a yellow, forty-three footer named *The Mixed Blessing*. Perfect for small groups and families. Tours starting at the end of April." He handed the man a business card. "If you youngsters happen to know anybody over the age of sixty be sure to let them know we've got a discount for seniors."

The old man laughed, as did his wife. "We'll keep an eye out for you."

Asher was so good at this, Peyton thought, he almost had her believing their life together was real, and not some pretend cover that would be over in days, one way or another. They reached the scuba shop and Asher opened the door for her.

"After you," he said.

The three of them stepped inside. The store was well maintained, airy and beautiful, with a family of mannequins in wet suits in the front and colorful fabric fish and seaweed hanging from the ceiling. Peyton hadn't exactly ever stopped to think about what she'd expect a business that operated a front for a drug operation to look like. But if she was honest, she would've imagined a dingy dry cleaning business, filthy dive bar or convenience store with half-empty shelves. But nothing like this. Judging by the number of people who'd recommended the place, it seemed Gunther's Scuba Shop had an excellent reputation. And it was hard to get her head around how someone could pour so much attention and care into their business and then jeopardize it by running drugs on the side.

A woman stood behind the counter. She was slender, muscular and tanned, with a silvery-white pixie cut. She wore an oversize sweatshirt hoodie over a white tank top. It fell loose off her shoulders, giving Peyton a glimpse of the intricate tattooed leaves and flowers that ran down her arms, where they disappeared under her sleeves. Peyton couldn't see her wrists.

"Can I help you?" the woman asked with a polite and professional smile.

Asher handed Peyton the end of Spark's leash and sauntered up to the desk.

"I'm Dan Johnson," Asher said. "This is my wife, Merry. Is Gunther here? I talked to him yesterday about renting some scuba equipment."

"No, sorry, my husband's not in this morning," she said. "But he left some gear aside for you, and I'm happy to help you guys out."

"Did he, now?" Asher asked.

Peyton noticed the woman didn't volunteer her name, but she knew from what Jasmin had told them that this must be Gunther's wife, Annika. Peyton explored the scuba shop while Asher stood at the desk and went over the equipment rental details with Annika. Silently Peyton instructed Spark to search. The dog's ears perked. Spark sniffed around the store but didn't signal. A wall of pictures near the back of the store commemorated Gunther's and Annika's bodybuilding days with pictures of them both hoisting weights and posing with medals and trophies.

Then she noticed a picture, which she guessed by Gunther's crisp tan suit and Annika's white linen dress was taken on their wedding day. They were standing by the water with a young man who she guessed was Annika's son, Finn. He looked a lot like his mother. Finn was frowning, his tie was undone, and his sleeves were pushed up to show an array of nautical and wildlife tattoos. His arms were so tightly crossed she couldn't see his wrists either. But he definitely had the same build as their masked attacker from the night before. More so than his mother did.

Judging by the picture, Finn wasn't all that impressed with his mother's second husband. Was Annika's son the one running the drug business? Was he working with Gunther? Trying to sabotage him?

"Is that your son?" Asher asked. He gestured to the picture Peyton was looking at, and she realized he must've been watching her and Spark out of the corner of his eye.

"Yes," Annika said.

"Did you rope him into the family business too?" Asher asked.

"Not so much," Annika said. She slid what looked like a hefty rental agreement across the counter for him to sign. "How about you? Do you two have any kids? We start children's classes at age ten, and they can get their scuba certification at twelve."

"No, no kids yet," Asher said with a casual smile. "But if it was up to the wife, we'd have five or six of them plus a bunch of dogs and cats."

He chuckled, but Peyton inhaled sharply, feeling as if a sudden burst of cold air had just overwhelmed her lungs. She'd told him that in confidence. She'd opened up and been vulnerable with him. And he'd just tossed her personal admission around to build rapport with a stranger. Asher's eyebrows rose as if he could tell something had rattled her. She broke his gaze and kept walking toward the back of the store and the change rooms.

Asher asked Annika if she and Gunther were planning on having any more kids, and when she laughed in response he added, "How about dogs?"

"My husband is not a big fan of dogs," Annika said. "Can't stand having them in the house, and only tolerates having them in the store because he doesn't want to lose customers."

A metal door lay ahead on Peyton's right. Spark turned toward it and woofed.

"You can take him out through that way if you want," Annika added.

Despite Asher's best attempts to distract Annika in conversation, it seemed like nothing got past her. Peyton pushed the heavy door open. She and Spark stepped outside into a back alley connected to the same maze of alleys that she'd found herself in the day before. Spark's snout rose as he sniffed the air. He walked a few steps in one direction, turned and went back the other, then he stopped and sat down in defeat. His ears drooped.

"It's okay, buddy," she said and scratched him behind the ears. "We're all just doing the best we can."

She found the door that they'd come through had automatically locked behind them. So, she followed the maze of alleys back around to the front of the store, where she found Asher waiting for her with a large hard-case bag of scuba gear on wheels. They started walking back down the boardwalk to *The Mixed Blessing* with Asher pulling the gear and Peyton holding Spark's leash.

Asher waited until they were three or four storefronts away from the scuba shop, glanced around to make sure nobody was close enough to overhear them, and then asked if she and Spark had found anything.

"Sadly, no," she said. "Just a lingering scent Spark couldn't trace."

"I got nothing from Annika either," he said. "I don't know about you, but I sure am tired of dead ends." He pulled out his phone and glanced at it. "We'll drop the gear at the boat, meet up with Tanner and then hit the water."

Spark growled softly. The dog's hackles rose. Without missing a beat, Asher held up his phone like he was taking a selfie of them, the camera clicked, then he lowered it and showed Peyton the picture on the screen. He'd taken a picture of the top of their heads, and the familiar shapes of Vaughan and Ridges were walking about fifteen paces behind them.

"Don't look now," Asher said. "But it looks like we're being followed."

# SEVEN

A shiver ran down Peyton's spine. She reached down and brushed her hand along Spark's neck, thanking the dog for letting them know about the two thugs on their tail.

"Now what?" she asked Asher softly.

"Well, I'm definitely not going to meet up with Tanner until we've lost them," he said. "He'll no doubt be dressed in street clothes, but they could try to tail him or target him, and adding another person into Merry and Dan's life will complicate our cover story."

"So what do we do?"

"Either we try to lose them," he said with a sigh, "or we wait them out. Hopefully they're just checking up on us to report back to whoever they're working for and won't trail us forever."

"I guess hopping in the boat and trying to outrun them is out of the question?" she asked.

"Not unless we want them to suddenly decide we're worth chasing," Asher said. "I'm still hoping they'll think Dan is somebody worth doing business with. That means our not doing anything suspicious and continuing to act like we've got nothing to hide. So, no ducking, no running and no weird actions that raise their suspicion. I'm still hoping yesterday's fake drug run was a test to make sure we'd follow instructions. If so, this might just all be part of the dance."

They lugged their equipment to *The Mixed Blessing*, stowed the scuba equipment below deck and made some awkward small talk for a while in the hopes Vaughan and Ridges would lose interest. But when they finally emerged there were Vaughan and Ridges, leaning against the railing halfway down the pier.

"Well, guess we've got some more time to kill," Asher said. "I'll let Tanner know we need a bit more time."

He fired a text off to Tanner and then took Spark's leash. Peyton looked at the sky. It was blue, but dark clouds had begun to arrive on the horizon. They didn't have all day. They strode back down the boardwalk. Asher nodded to the men as they passed.

Asher and Peyton walked in silence for a while, checking out the street artists, vendors and stalls.

"Are we okay?" Asher asked, after a long moment. "You looked kind of annoyed at me back in the scuba shop."

"Honestly?" Peyton felt her voice begin to rise and fought to keep it level. "I can't believe you told that woman that I wanted a whole bunch of kids. That was my personal business and not yours to share."

"I'm sorry," Asher said. "Sincerely. I should've realized that was out of line."

She could tell that he meant it.

"Okay," she said. "I'm just not as smooth as you at doing the whole charming act you do. I'm not good at shutting myself off behind a smile and hiding what I'm thinking and feeling like you are."

She'd said the words lightly enough, and yet she watched as something dark flashed across his eyes.

"What's wrong?" she asked.

"Nothing," he said.

"Yeah, right."

Asher swallowed hard. Then he stopped walking, took her hand and pulled her closer to him. His head bent toward her as if he was about to kiss her cheek. Instead he stopped a few inches from her face, his sad green eyes met hers and when he spoke his voice barely rose above a whisper. "Dan Johnson reminds me of my father. I modeled Dan's confidence and swagger on him."

Pain pierced her heart. She watched as a world of hurt filled his gaze.

Impulsively, her free hand reached up and brushed the side of his face. "I'm so sorry."

"Me too."

They stood there for a long moment on the boardwalk, feeling people pass by and break around them like waves. Then Asher blew out a long breath, he pulled away and they kept walking.

*Lord, I wish there was something I could do to help him. I want to heal his hurt about his father and his mother. I want to go find his sister, Mara, and bring her safely home. I know You love Asher and understand his pain. Bring him healing and hope.*

Then she glanced back. Vaughan and Ridges were still on their tail. Asher followed her gaze and sighed.

They spent the next hour wandering down the boardwalk, passing out business cards for their pretend boating tours and greeting more strangers. They wandered in and out of Rock River's three tattoo parlors, where Asher charmed the staff and told them all about their plans for the tour operation they were launching in the spring, Peyton scanned the walls and binders of artwork for anything that matched the lines they'd seen on the man's arm, and Spark subtly sniffed for drugs. But all three were dead ends. What's worse was that they hadn't managed to shake their unwanted shadows.

Clearly they needed another strategy. Tanner couldn't just hang around nearby waiting to meet up forever, and once the rain hit with a vengeance it wouldn't be safe to dive.

Peyton, Asher and Spark stopped in front of a large community wall mural and pretended to admire the painting and ignore the fact Vaughan and Ridges were lingering by the railing just a few feet away.

"Now what?" she whispered.

"If we had unlimited time, I'd say we call it a day and go back to the lodge," Asher said. "But unfortunately we don't have that luxury."

The longer the case dragged on, the higher the risk that whoever had the bloodhounds would move them to another location. If they were even still there at all. Not to mention there were only going to be a few more good days of weather for boating and swimming before the rainy season hit and they'd have to pack the whole mission up.

But for better or for worse, Asher's Dan Johnson radiated a tense and urgent energy that implied something interesting was about to go down. Oddly it almost reminded her of how the PNK9 kennel got whenever somebody walked in crinkling a bag of potato chips. And while it was a really good quality when they wanted to attract the wrong type of attention and had led to getting their first solid bite yesterday, the trick now was to convince the very same predators that there was nothing to see here.

"So we need to convince them that Dan's not about to do anything interesting today?" she asked. "You think that'll work?"

"That's my hunch."

She scanned the boardwalk. Her eyes alit on the caricaturist farther down past where Vaughan and Ridges stood. She reached for Asher's hand, looped her fingers through his and gave his hand a tug.

"Come on," she said. "I got an idea that's so silly it just might work. Follow my lead."

Asher hesitated, then he nodded. "Got it."

She kept hold of his hand and the three of them started to walk down the boardwalk toward the caricaturist. The man had a gray ponytail and was dressed in a flowy orange smock. The boards beside him were covered with colorful sketches he'd done of the tourists and boats in the harbor. A sign at the side of his easel advertised a single original sketch for twenty-five dollars apiece or a trio of three sketches on the same page for fifty. Perfect.

She leaned her head toward him.

"Okay," she whispered. "This time when we pass our unwanted friends, stop and look at them with your best Dan Johnson stare."

His left eyebrow rose. She could tell he wanted an explanation. But her plan didn't involve pausing long enough to give him one. So instead she ignored the question in his eyes, broke his gaze and strode confidently down the boardwalk with the stride that exuded every bit as much confidence as her pretend husband's did. They drew closer to Vaughan and Ridges. Doubt stuttered in her heart. Was this actually going to work?

Right on cue, Asher turned and glared at the men as if he was moments away from walking over and popping one of them in the jaw. He pulled away from her hand and took a step toward them.

Quickly, Peyton stepped in front of Asher and grabbed both of his hands in hers.

"Don't!" she said sharply, letting her voice rise, hoping that even if the men weren't able to catch all of the words, her body language would broadcast Merry's frustrations with her husband loud and clear. "Enough of this! It's bad enough we wasted hours yesterday running on whatever foolish goose chase you all think you got going on. I'm not going to let you waste today too. This trip was supposed to be a second chance at having a proper honeymoon. You promised me that today was going to be all about you and me!"

Asher's eyes widened. His mouth opened and closed again as if he was struggling to figure out what she even said.

"I'm sorry, buttercup," he stammered. "I didn't mean…"

"You want me to take the dog and go back to our hotel?" she demanded. "Because you know I will. It has a really nice pool and a spa."

She pulled her hands away from his.

"Don't be ridiculous, darling," he tried again.

"I knew I shouldn't have let you talk me into combining a honeymoon with work." She took a step back and waved both hands in the air. "My mother warned me that this would happen!"

Asher grabbed both of her hands and brought them to his lips, and she realized he was trying to hide a smile.

"I said I was sorry," he said. He brushed his mouth over her knuckles. The pretend act of tenderness sent very real chills up her arms. "How can I fix this?"

"I want honeymoon pictures," she said.

He shrugged. "Fine."

She looped her arm through Asher's, smiled triumphantly and led him and Spark over to the caricaturist. She didn't dare look Vaughan and Ridges's way until she reached the artist and was happy to see the men had retreated a way down the boardwalk. Seemed they didn't want to get involved in a marital spat. Good. Now to see just how much time they were prepared to waste watching Dan and Merry doing absolutely nothing interesting or suspicious, before giving up and moving on. After all, every moment Vaughan and Ridges were watching them do boring couple stuff was a moment they weren't searching for their missing drugs.

"We'd like the three sketch package, please," she told the caricaturist, brightly. "I'm Merry, this is my husband, Dan, and this is Spark."

The dog wagged his tail in greeting.

"Is there an extra cost to include the dog in the sketches?" Asher asked.

The artist told them he'd include the dog for another ten. He added that the initial session would take about twenty minutes and they could come back later in the day to pick up the completed sketches. Then he directed Asher to sit on a stool and Peyton to sit on his knee. He set up a crate for Spark to sit on and for Peyton to rest her feet on. Spark waited patiently for Asher and Peyton to get settled, then the dog hopped up on the crate and sat obediently. Asher wrapped one strong arm behind Peyton's back to steady her. He was so close that she could smell him filling her senses. It reminded her of coffee, the forest, burning embers and home.

"So, tell me a little bit about yourselves," the caricaturist said.

"We got married this summer and this is our official honeymoon," Peyton said. "We're based in Canada and were hoping to start a cross-border tour boat business in the spring. I'm American originally. Our boat's called *The Mixed Blessing*. We bought it secondhand from my cousin and cleaned it up. It's perfect for small groups and families."

"Mmm-hmm," the artist said. His eyes glanced from them to the paper in front of him and back to them again. "Can you guys get a little closer? Maybe you could lean against his shoulder?"

She did as he suggested. Asher's arm tightened around her. She felt the scruff of his beard brush against her cheek.

"Looking good," the caricaturist said. "What was your wedding like?"

"Really simple," Peyton said, remembering

the story she'd written in the stolen journal. "We got married in a friend's backyard."

"Were there flowers?" the artist asked.

"Roses," she said. "Red ones. They're my favorite."

"Everyone got all dressed up?" he asked.

"Dan wore a suit and I wore a dress," she said. "But most of our friends just wore jeans. We had burgers and hotdogs on the barbecue after."

"Sounds nice," the caricaturist said. "Could you guys turn to face each other now?"

"It was really nice," Peyton said. She looked up into Asher's face. He was staring deeply into her eyes. "One of the things I really appreciate about this man is how deeply he cares about the things that actually matter and never wants to waste time worrying about things that don't. A lot of brides would get upset that the groom didn't care about the flowers or the table settings. But it was the opposite for me. I love that he focuses on the important stuff and ignores the rest. It makes me feel safe."

"Really?" Asher asked. She could feel his breath on her face. And for a moment she couldn't tell if he was asking as himself or as Dan.

"Yeah, really," she said. "I really like that about you."

"Now, Dan, if you could lean forward a bit like you're going to give your wife a little kiss," the artist said, and she realized for a moment she'd almost forgotten that he was there. "Wonderful. Closer."

Asher leaned in, Peyton felt her eyes close then suddenly their lips met. The kiss was sweet and so gentle that she barely felt his lips on hers as she kissed him back.

"All good. I think I got everything we need," the artist said. "I should have the sketches for you in an hour or two."

Peyton opened her eyes and pulled back. So did Asher. His face paled as if he'd been just as shocked by the unexpected kiss as she'd been. How had it happened? Which one of them had initiated the kiss? Had it just been an accident? If so, why had neither of them stopped it? She took a few steps away from Asher down the boardwalk, putting as much distance as she could between herself and what had just happened moments before. Her eyes drifted over the sketches the artist had laid out on the boards, as she fought to settle her heart and calm her breath.

There were rowboats, sailboats, motorboats and dazzling blue water. Then suddenly a flash of gold, brown and black caught her attention. She bent down and looked closer. There in bright and energetic lines was a drawing of three bloodhound puppies in a motorboat. They were standing with their paws up against the side. Their long ears flapped in the breeze. Their noses rose toward the sunrise.

She snatched up the picture and stared.

It was Agent, Ranger and Chief.

It was her three missing puppies. They were here.

Asher's heart beat like a marching band had both taken over his chest and started clanging cymbals in his ears. He stood and glanced down the boardwalk. Peyton's plan to convince Vaughan and Ridges that there was nothing interesting to see here had worked. He'd spotted the two men shrug and wander off partway through the art session and were nowhere in sight.

But at what cost to his jangled nerves?

He'd never just gone and spontaneously kissed someone before. Let alone someone like Peyton—the most fascinating, interesting, kind, thoughtful and not to mention downright beautiful woman he had ever laid his eyes on.

What had he been thinking? What must she think of him?

He could feel Spark nuzzling against his hand silently, asking him what was wrong, and was vaguely aware of the artist's voice telling him when to come back later.

"Danny, honey!" Peyton called, cutting through his chaotic thoughts. "Come look at these bloodhound puppies!"

Bloodhound puppies?

The words snapped him back to reality. He turned to look at the large sketch she held in her hand. There they were, clear as day, three puppies in a boat. It was hard to tell anything concrete from the sketch, but they definitely seemed a few months older than the bloodhounds had been when they were taken.

Were these their missing dogs?

"Well." Asher struggled for words. "That's not something you see every day."

"Aren't they the cutest?" the caricaturist asked. "Couldn't much believe my eyes when I saw them out on the water and sketched them down as quickly as I could."

"You actually saw these puppies?" Peyton asked. "Here?"

"Yup, I sure did."

"When?" Peyton asked.

"Just this morning."

"What time?" she pressed.

"Well, I don't know, sometime around sunrise, I guess," he said, "judging by the fact the sun is rising in the picture. I just saw them for a second. If it's not in the picture I don't remember it."

"So, you don't remember who was driving the boat?" Peyton asked. "Was it a man or woman? Young or old?"

The caricaturist shrugged. Asher stepped next to Peyton and softly squeezed her arm, to warn that her questions were getting dangerously close to raising suspicion.

"My wife is absolutely crazy about dogs," Asher said, with a smile. "How much for the picture?"

"Give me an extra ten and we'll call it even," the caricaturist said.

"Deal," Asher said. He pulled a twenty and a fifty from his wallet to cover the session. It had been a pricey detour but a pretty effective one.

Then Asher, Peyton and Spark continued walking down the boardwalk. Asher was holding the leash again, and Peyton clutched the picture to her chest as if she was holding the puppies themselves.

"Are you sure it's them?" he asked.

"I am," she said. Tears filled her eyes.

The fact she was certain was good enough for him. They'd been right. The stolen puppies had been here in this very area just hours ago.

He prayed and thanked God.

Then he reached over and ran a supportive

hand over the top of Peyton's back, in between her shoulder blades.

"We're close," he said, "and we're going to find them and bring them home safe."

Her hazel eyes met his and he felt something tighten in his chest. He stepped back and looked away. He couldn't let himself be emotionally compromised by her. No matter what might've thumped inside his heart when he'd foolishly kissed her lips.

The three of them walked in aimless circles around the boardwalk and marina for a good thirty minutes, while he scanned for any sign of the men who'd been trailing them. But they were nowhere to be seen. Hopefully they'd given up and reported back to whomever they were working for that Dan and Merry Johnson weren't up to anything worth spying on today. Asher texted Jasmin to see if she could find any trace of Vaughan and Ridges on security or traffic cameras, and a few minutes later she texted back that she'd spotted two men matching their description hopping in a truck and heading down the highway to Port Angeles.

That was good enough for Asher. He texted Tanner and a few moments later they met up in a quiet alley behind a florist.

Spark and Britta wagged their tails in greeting. Asher handed Tanner Spark's leash.

"Thanks again for taking him for a bit," Asher said, "and for your patience. After what happened yesterday, I don't like the idea of leaving him alone on the boat."

"No problem," Tanner said. "It's a nice town."

Yeah, it was just too bad it had a drug smuggling problem. Hopefully, they wouldn't just find the missing puppies but also help take a bite out of the local drug scene while they were at it.

"I'm sure Spark will enjoy the hike," Peyton said. "He's been pretty patient about spending so much time on the job and following us around." She held out the picture to show him. "We think we have a lead."

Tanner chuckled then stopped himself.

"Sorry," he said. "It's kind of a goofy picture, the way their big ears are flapping and their tongues are waggling."

"Yeah, you're right, it is," Peyton said. "Maybe I'll frame it and hang it in my office when this is all over." A smile crossed her lips and unshed tears brushed her eyes. "As much as I hate to let it go, I was hoping you could take it to Jasmin. I know it's just a cartoon and not a photograph. But maybe the caricaturist picked up something helpful without him realizing, like the model of the boat or the direction it was headed."

"Absolutely," Tanner said and took the picture almost reverently as if it was a priceless Picasso.

"While you're at it," Peyton added, "would you mind digging a little deeper into Gunther's Scuba Shop and seeing if there's anything there? Judging by the picture I saw of Annika's wedding to Gunther on the wall, I get the impression the relationship between stepfather and stepson is kind of rocky. Jasmin said she'd seen indications there was no love lost between them."

"Will do," Tanner said.

Asher ran his hand over Spark's back and told him to have fun. Then Tanner and the dogs headed toward an unmarked police SUV, which Asher assumed he'd borrowed for the day. Asher and Peyton headed back to *The Mixed Blessing*.

He wasn't quite sure why he'd automatically assumed he'd pilot the boat. But instead he stepped back as Peyton took the helm. She was uncharacteristically quiet as *The Mixed Blessing* pulled out of the Rock River marina, and they made their way down the coast to the cove near Salt Creek where they'd been shot at the day before.

Somehow he found himself missing her smile.

"It's too bad they haven't created scuba gear

for dogs," he said. "Because I'm sure Spark would love being down there with us with a little mask and flippers on."

She nodded as if she hadn't heard him.

"Are you okay?" he asked.

"I'm just thinking about the puppies," she said. "It's been almost four months since they were stolen. What if they don't remember me? What if they're no longer the happy and smart little dogs that they once were?"

He felt the urge to hug her. But he didn't know how his heart would react to feeling her that close to his chest. So instead he shrugged.

"I don't know," he said. "But I have faith in you. If anyone can find those dogs, retrain them to join the PNK9 and help them remember who they once were, it's you."

They dropped anchor and took turns going below deck to change. He'd gotten Peyton a wet suit with a hood, so that she'd be able to take off her wig and keep her hair safely hidden inside. They checked the rented equipment carefully for any sign of tampering or damage. Then they geared up, and he watched as Peyton stood on the edge of the diving platform, steadied her air regulator in her mouth and stepped out boldly into the water. A moment later she emerged and gave him a thumbs-up. He signaled her back, then he joined her in the water.

Peace swept over Asher as he let his body sink underneath the surface. The water was an unbelievable shade of deep green that grew to a dark blue the deeper he swam. Towering seaweed forests rose around him, filled with dozens upon dozens of fish. The coast of Olympic National Park was created by dark layers of glacial rock that had been beat up against the shore by the powerful waves of the Pacific Ocean, until it formed jagged cliffs and stunning sea stacks that rose like pillars out of the water. It was stunning.

He felt his heartbeat settle. The sound of his own breath filled his ears. For the first time in years his body felt weightless and free from all the burdens and stress that weighed him down.

*Lord*, he prayed. *What would it be like for my heart to feel this free? Forgive me for how I've let everything I'm carrying impact my work, my colleagues, my family and the people around me. Help me find this kind of peace, every day in You.*

Together he and Peyton explored the rugged coastline, swimming into deep chasms and narrow channels, but never finding a cave inside large enough for the bottles of drugs to be hidden inside.

Finally, he gave up and signaled to Peyton that it was time to go. She signaled back in agreement, and they began to swim back toward *The Mixed Blessing.*

He was still several yards behind her when a flurry of bubbles shook the water ahead. A vessel was coming. It was small and fast.

There was a splash. Then suddenly he saw a figure in a black wet suit and goggles swimming for Peyton. She turned. The man grabbed at Peyton's head as if trying to pull the air regulator from her mouth or the mask from her face, while she thrashed and struggled against him.

*Peyton!*

Desperately Asher swam toward her.

Then the masked man grabbed Peyton around the throat. A knife flashed in his hand.

# EIGHT

Something white-hot and protective burned through Asher's veins, as he saw Peyton bravely battling for her life against her attacker.

*Get away from her!*

The words welled up inside him far more powerfully than anything his voice would've been able to shout. He sped through the water, pushing and pulling as hard as he could with every stroke. Peyton wrenched free from the masked man and tried to swim for the surface. Peyton's attacker grabbed her by the ankle. She thrashed wildly.

But now Asher had reached them. He grabbed the guy by his oxygen tank and yanked him back. Peyton wriggled her leg free and swam toward the boat. The masked man wrestled out of Asher's grasp and spun back. He swung the knife at Asher with a sudden burst of ferocity and Asher caught sight of the jagged lines of a tattoo on his wrist. Being underwater made it almost feel as if everything was happening in slow motion and distorted the scene before Asher's eyes. And yet there was no mistaking the man's intentions as he tried to stab at him again and again—wild, vicious and uncontrollable swings as Asher struggled to block the blows.

Asher took a breath and choked. His air supply had been cut off. Water trickled in through his regulator mouthpiece. How? They'd checked the equipment carefully. Had his attacker brought a weapon sharp enough to pierce his air hose?

Either way, Asher had lost his ability to breathe. Panic filled his chest. If he didn't get air soon Asher was going to drown. Desperately he tried to swim toward the sun streaming down from above. But his attacker loomed over him and wouldn't let him go.

Asher's lungs burned. He fought the urge to inhale, knowing that if he let water pour into his lungs it could be his death. Bright dots started to fill his eyes.

Then he saw a flurry of orange streaming down from above him, catching the trickling beams of sunlight like underwater fire. It was Peyton. Some of her hair had slipped free from a large hole in the back of her hood and was now fanning out around her. She swam for their attacker.

No. He wouldn't let her risk her life. He couldn't let her die. Not for him.

He watched as she grabbed the attacker from behind, wrapped her arms around his neck and yanked the regulator from his mouth. The man shook Peyton off of him and swam for his watercraft.

Peyton grabbed Asher's hand and started swimming, half guiding and half pulling him after her, and aiming for the surface on the other side of *The Mixed Blessing* from where their attacker had gone. But it was too late. Asher had gone too long without oxygen. His limbs were heavy and sluggish. He could feel his mind beginning to go dark. His hand slipped from her grasp. Asher's eyes closed.

He was going to drown.

Then he felt Peyton grip the front of his suit. Hard rubber pressed up against his mouth.

"Asher!" Peyton's distorted voice shouted at him through the water. "Take it!"

He opened his eyes to see her staring intently into his face. She was holding her breath and trying to force him to take her air regulator mouthpiece in his mouth, offering him her oxygen. He tried to shake his head. But something firm in her hazel eyes told him she'd risk drowning before she saved herself and left him there.

*Oh, Peyton, I don't deserve you.*

He expelled as much water as he could from his mouth, then took her mouthpiece and breathed deeply. Relief exploded through his core as he felt the life-giving air fill his lungs. Fresh energy surged through his limbs. The sound of a motor filtered above them through the water. He looked to see their masked attacker's watercraft streaming away. Thankfully they weren't that deep underwater, otherwise they'd have been in even more serious trouble, especially if they'd tried to surface quickly. He reached to return the regulator to Peyton, but she shook her head and instead took his hand. Side by side they swam for the surface, until he felt her begin to struggle. Then he stopped and handed her the mouthpiece back again. This time she accepted it and took a deep breath. Together they rose through the water, sharing her oxygen and passing the regulator back and forth between them.

He broke through the surface with Peyton beside him. Their attacker was nowhere to be seen. They made their way to the boat. He let her climb up the ladder first and then went up after her.

She wriggled out of her air tank and collapsed onto the deck. He did so too, with his flippered feet still dangling over the end of the diving platform. For a long moment they lay there, gasping and panting for breath.

Asher found his voice first. "You saved my life."

She dragged herself up to sitting and he did likewise.

"No problem," she said. "You'd have done the same for me."

She pulled her mask off, taking with it the remains of her wet suit's damaged hood. He pulled his mask off as well.

"What happened to your hood?" he asked.

"He ripped it while we were fighting," she said. "But my hair didn't come loose until I was swimming back for you. I don't think he did it on purpose. I think he was just trying to drag me up to the surface. How did he cut off your oxygen?"

"I don't know," Asher said. He ran his hand along the air hose until he found a small nick in the rubber barely a quarter of an inch wide. He held it up to show her. "He was stabbing pretty wildly. Maybe he caught the hose by accident. Then again, his knife had to be incredibly sharp to pierce the hose, so maybe it was intentional." He blew out a long breath. "Honestly, everything happened so fast, I was just trying to survive."

"He wanted to kill you," Peyton said. Her

voice choked in her throat. Tears rushed to the corners of her hazel eyes. "I thought you weren't going to make it."

"Hey, it's okay," Asher said. He reached for her hand. She took it and gripped him tightly. "We're both okay. We're both still here. Thanks to your quick thinking."

For a long moment they sat there in the back of *The Mixed Blessing*, with their fingers linked and his gaze lost in her eyes. Silence fell except for the sound of water lapping up against the hull and trees dancing in the wind.

Then she pulled her hand away and brushed strands of hair off her face.

"Did you see the tattoo on his wrist?" she asked.

"I did," he said.

"It was him, again," she said. "This was the third time he's tried to attack us."

And now he'd seen Peyton's red hair.

The October sun had already started its slow descent toward the horizon as *The Mixed Blessing* started its journey back to Rock River. They changed out of their wet suits, repacked their equipment back in the bag and Peyton repinned her wig and put her hat back on. Then they stood side by side at the helm, called the chief on video call and filled him in on what had happened.

Donovan was rightly concerned and asked them both pointedly if they wanted to continue with the undercover mission.

"Yes," Peyton had said quickly, before Asher could answer. "The puppies are here. Somebody saw them just this morning. We're so close. We can't give up now."

She turned to Asher and waited for him to agree with her. Instead, he ran his hand over his beard.

"I don't like the fact the attacker saw Peyton's real hair slip out through a large hole in her wet suit hood," Asher said. "But everything that happened in that moment was so chaotic I don't even know if he'd have noticed—"

"And even if he did, that's no reason to end the investigation," Peyton added.

"Honestly," Asher went on, "I'm more concerned about how dangerous this is all becoming and my ability to keep Peyton safe." To keep her safe? Peyton opened her mouth to interject. But before she could say a word Asher quickly added, "I mean, to keep us both safe."

The chief nodded noncommittally and said he'd see them later in the group video chat.

Peyton's heart was heavy as they docked

and made their way by foot to the alley where they'd arranged to meet up with Tanner. Clouds had begun to move in ahead and the tourists had disappeared for the day. Asher's brows were knit as well, and this time he didn't try to stop and chat up the tour business with the few boardwalk vendors they passed.

Thankfully, neither Vaughan nor Ridges were anywhere in sight.

"How do you suggest we deal with things at Gunther's?" she asked. "They're going to notice we're returning damaged equipment."

"Depends on whether it's Gunther or Annika behind the counter," Asher said. His frown deepened and he didn't meet her gaze. "Leave it with me. I'll come up with something."

As they reunited with Spark, the dog softly nuzzled Peyton's hand as if sensing something was wrong. Unmistakable concern filled Tanner's eyes.

"I heard what happened," Tanner said. "You guys okay?"

"We're fine," Peyton said. Her chin rose. "Just more determined than ever to find the puppies and catch the people behind all this."

They said goodbye to Tanner and Britta, and made their way on foot down the boardwalk back to the scuba shop, with Peyton holding Spark's leash and Asher dragging the roller bag containing scuba gear. She'd completely forgotten about the caricatures they'd done until the artist called out to them. He'd sketched all three onto one extra-large piece of paper. Asher thanked him kindly, rolled it up and tucked it under one arm.

When they got to the scuba shop, Annika was still there, leaning against the front counter and looking tired.

"We had a problem," Asher said bluntly and loudly, the moment they stepped into the store. "My air hose snagged on something sharp and Merry got a tear in her wet suit. Seems diving is a dangerous business around here."

Annika stood up straight. Her eyes widened. It was the first glimpse of real, genuine and unguarded emotion that Peyton had seen from her. Asher hoisted the heavy bag of wet equipment up onto the counter in front of her, unzipped it and showed her the wet suit and hose.

"Now, I don't want any trouble," Asher added. His hand waved as if graciously declining an offer that she hadn't even made. "We're trying to build our own business here and we value our cooperation with other local businesses, especially one with such a great reputation as yourselves. So, how about we say you keep the two-hundred-dollar damage deposit we paid when we rented these, and we'll just chalk it up to just one of those things?"

Annika still hadn't answered. Instead, she ran her hands over the damaged air hose. Annika saw the cut the knife had made, and Peyton watched as something changed in the woman's eyes.

"Where were you when this happened?" Annika asked.

There was an edge to her voice that Peyton hadn't heard there before.

It was like Annika was worried. Or even afraid.

But of what? Of the fact they'd been attacked? Of whoever attacked them?

"We were looking for some underwater caves," Asher said.

"Where?" Annika asked.

"Near Salt Creek," Asher said. "We were exploring the coast."

"The coast," Annika repeated.

"Yup," Asher said.

The woman blinked and in an instant the professional look was back.

"I'm sorry this happened," she said. "This looks like it was caused by normal wear and tear to me. I appreciate your discretion. I'll be happy to refund your rental cost and put a credit for your next rental on the books for you."

"Why, that's extremely and unexpectedly kind of you," Asher said.

For a long moment, Asher and the scuba shop owner stared at each other like two gunslingers waiting to see if the other would blink. Peyton glanced at Spark. The dog wasn't signaling. Spark didn't smell anything off. Then Asher turned toward the door.

"Well, thanks again," he said. "I'm sure we'll be seeing you soon."

Asher, Peyton and Spark were almost to the door when suddenly Annika's voice came from behind them.

"The reason I asked where this occurred," Annika called, "is I was wondering if you'd checked out Lake Crescent."

The three of them stopped and turned back.

"No," Asher said. "Never heard if it."

"Lake Crescent is inside Olympic National Park," Annika said. "Only very small boats are allowed. You'd have to rent one, a truck and a trailer to get there."

So, there was no way any drug-filled bottles thrown overboard in the Salish Sea could've floated there.

"The lake is a bit off the beaten path," Annika added. "But it's known for having the best diving and most interesting caves around. It's my son Finn's favorite spot."

"Thank you," Asher said. "We'll keep that in mind."

They left the store and walked back to the marina, picking up a couple of pizzas on their way for dinner. It wasn't until they were back on board *The Mixed Blessing* that Asher asked Peyton, "What's your take on Annika?"

"That comment at the end about Lake Crescent almost sounded like she was trying to help us," Peyton said.

"Agreed," Asher said. "The question is why and with what."

"I thinks she suspects that you were lying about the damage to our gear," Peyton said. "But I don't know if we're going to get her to tell us what she thinks might've really happened to it."

"Agreed again," Asher said. "But she might've been trying to nudge us somewhere."

To help them? Or to get them into deeper trouble?

This time when they got back to their suite at the lodge, Asher insisted that Peyton wait in the hallway with Spark and the pizzas, while he went inside and did a quick search to make sure there weren't any unwanted visitors or unpleasant surprises. But everything was exactly as they'd left it, including the small tower of pennies Asher had strategically placed on the other side of the main door and the pencil he'd left on the top of the door to the bedroom.

Once they were all inside the suite, Asher dropped the rolled-up picture he'd gotten from the caricaturist on the couch and went to refill Spark's water dish. Peyton unrolled the picture and looked at it. There were three sketches of various sizes on the same page. The first showed the three of them in a boat with Spark in a captain's hat. The second picture was the three of them as a mermaid, merman and merdog surrounded by bubbles. The third was Merry and Dan kissing on their wedding day. Spark held a bouquet of roses in his mouth.

A sudden lump rose in her throat. Why was she tormenting herself by looking at pictures of the happy life they'd never have when there were so many more important things she should be thinking about?

They ate their pizza in awkward silence as they waited for the team meeting to begin. This time Asher and Peyton sat at opposite ends of the crescent-shaped couch. They'd each been on their own laptop when the call had started, and neither of them had moved to join the other. So she could see Asher both in a small box on the screen in front of her and also in person when she looked up over her computer. Spark leaped onto the couch and curled up beside Asher. The dog's head bobbed in and out of the frame.

Tanner, Veronica, Owen and Jasmin were all on the call, like they'd been the day before, with Chief Donovan hosting.

"Glad to see everyone," Donovan said. "I'm especially glad to see that Asher and Peyton are doing well after your ordeal earlier."

"Yup," Asher said. "No worse for wear, thankfully." As if being attacked underwater by a knife-wielding assailant was no different than tripping and stubbing his toe. "We'll be even better when we catch whoever's behind this and find the dogs."

"Thankfully, we now know for certain the bloodhound puppies are in Rock River," Peyton said. "Or at least they were here this morning."

"I've been analyzing the picture of them you got from the caricaturist," Jasmin said.

Peyton leaned forward, hoping for some good news.

"No results on the tattoo front yet," Owen interjected. He must've been sitting close to the microphone because she heard a high-pitched whine fill the speaker. She quickly slid her headphones on and turned off her speaker to avoid any echo from the fact she and Asher were both on their computers in the same room. Asher glanced her way then silently did likewise.

"We talked to over fifty tattoo artists and didn't get anything," Owen went on. "It's just too bad we don't have more to go on than a couple of smudgy lines."

"Although one tattoo artist did say something that might be helpful," Veronica said. "She suggested the fact the lines were messy could mean the tattoo wasn't done professionally at all but by an amateur who just happened to get his hands on a tattoo gun."

"But of course we will keep looking into all possibilities," Owen said, "and the more information you guys on the ground can give us the better."

From the way Owen interrupted Jasmin and Veronica, again Peyton found herself wondering if Owen's eagerness to get a full-time slot on the team was getting in the way of his sense of teamwork.

"Jasmin, were you able to glean anything from the picture of the puppies?" Peyton asked.

"A couple things, yeah," Jasmin said. Peyton heard a keyboard click, then the box that had contained Jasmin's picture filled with the image of the puppies on the boat. "See these lines here?" A cursor arrow circled around a zigzag symbol on the hull. "That would be the logo of a Sapphire Crest model of motorboat, and the silver paint narrows it down to being sold in the last three years. Now, there have been thousands of boats of that model and color sold in North America, but only a few hundred in Washington State—and one was sold to Gunther's Scuba Shop and registered to Annika's son, Finn."

Asher whistled and leaned back against the couch. "Now, that is interesting."

"Though sadly not enough for a search warrant," Tanner added.

"Maybe not," Jasmin said. "But if I triangulate the height of the figure at the wheel with the size of the boat and the relative distance to the sunrise, my best guess is that whoever was driving was broad shouldered and somewhere between five foot five and five foot eight."

"Which matches both Gunther and his wife," Asher said. "Possibly Finn."

"But which from an evidentiary standpoint is also meaningless," the chief added, "as caricaturists aren't exactly known for being sticklers about shape and proportion. I agree that it's interesting but still not enough to get us a warrant."

It was like building a tower of matchsticks, Peyton thought. Eventually they'd get so many that the tower would fall.

"Were you able to gather anything more about the yacht that was smuggling cocaine in water bottles last spring?" Asher asked.

"Yes," Donovan said, "and it's not conclusive but it is promising. Law enforcement did not consider the European diplomat a suspect. They think the three-man crew used him as a dupe to try and smuggle drugs on his boat. There were only two crew members on board when the boat was raided, neither were arrested due to a lack of evidence and they're both in the wind. I'm trying to get pictures sent over. Again, I'm hoping to have more information about this tomorrow."

Peyton just hoped that the dogs wouldn't be moved to a new location by then.

"Tanner, did you find out anything about Gunther and Annika?" Peyton asked.

There had been something about the look in Annika's eyes back at the scuba shop that Peyton still hadn't been able to shake.

"Pretty much what I gather Jasmin told you the other day," Tanner said. "Although I've also now determined neither Gunther nor Annika has a license to carry a loaded gun or a history of buying or owning weapons. They have two properties, the store and the house. Gunther is the kind of man who believes speed limits don't apply to him, and as you already know, Annika took a restraining order out on her ex—"

"When was that?" Peyton interjected.

"Over a decade ago," Tanner said. "But one interesting thing a buddy did tip me off about is that Annika walked into a Seattle PD station sometime in June and tried to report her son, Finn, missing."

"What?" Asher asked. He sat up straight. Peyton did so at the same time, and the two of them looked across the room and their eyes met.

"You mean to tell me that police are already actively looking for Finn?" Asher asked.

Peyton thought of the tattooed young man who wasn't smiling in the pictures. Could he be the person who'd attacked them?

"Nah, police didn't even open a case file," Tanner said, "because he's a grown man in his twenties. Plus it really shot Annika's credibility when she showed them texts from her son's phone, after he 'went missing,' claiming he hated her and didn't want anything to do with her."

"But she believed something serious had happened to him?" Peyton asked.

Tanner nodded. "She did."

Once again Peyton met Asher's eyes.

"What are you thinking?" Asher asked.

"That we need to take a closer look at that family," Peyton said.

A puzzle was slowly beginning to form, but there were still too many pieces to know what they were seeing.

"Chief." Asher sat up straight and addressed Donovan. "I'm worried that time is running out on this case. Because of the time of year, there are only going to be a few more safe days for scuba diving this season, and the puppies could be moved to a new location at any moment. Maybe even in the next few hours. I'm requesting permission to mount a full-on stakeout operation on Gunther's home, tonight."

# NINE

Peyton held her breath as Donovan paused and considered Asher's request. She was still rattled at the fact the chief had asked earlier in the day if they should just ditch the whole investigation. Peyton closed her eyes and prayed.

"Okay, what's the plan?" Donovan said.

Asher suggested that he and Tanner go alone with their K-9 partners, while Peyton stay back at the lodge. She wasn't sure if Donovan had noticed the immediate frustration she'd felt flash across her face, but the chief quickly shot that down.

"I think it's best that you and Peyton stay completely out of sight," Donovan said. "I want you both watching from a distance in case anything goes down. If officers do need to move in I don't want you to blow your cover. We'll have Tanner and Jackson on the ground with the candidates. It'll be a good opportunity to assess them."

Peyton held her breath waiting for Asher to argue, but he didn't and within moments the details were hammered out and settled. Gunther and Annika's home was set deep in the woods on a narrow and unpaved rural road. Tanner, his K-9 partner, Britta, Owen and Veronica would form one ground surveillance team, while Jackson and his Doberman partner, Rex, would form a second with Parker and Brandie.

Meanwhile, Asher, Peyton and Spark would be stationed a safe distance away on a hill overlooking the operation with binoculars. They'd be close enough to see everything that was going on, but far enough away that their cover wouldn't be blown if things went down.

The call was ended, and then Peyton and Asher busied themselves checking their laptops and phones and making stilted small talk as they got ready for their stakeout. An odd and uncomfortable silence filled the suite that was worlds away from the ease and comfort she'd felt sitting with him on the couch the night before, watching the flames dance in the fireplace and listening to the rain pattering outside. It was like that inexplicable and unexpected kiss they'd shared on the boardwalk had detonated something between them and the scent still lingered in the air. She wanted to get back to the easy camaraderie they had before but wasn't quite sure how. Asher's brows were knit and his forehead creased as if his thoughts were locked away in a mental prison of his own making.

It was just before midnight when they left the lodge and found the unmarked and dark green SUV that Jasmin had arranged for them in a parking lot by the marina. Clouds had moved in, blocking out the stars and filling the air with the smell of impending rain. They drove in silence to a quiet spot above Gunther and Annika's home, keeping their headlights off for the last twenty minutes of the journey. They parked and cut the engine on the edge of a small cliff and looked down through the darkness at the quiet house below.

Asher raised his walkie-talkie to his mouth.

"It's Asher. We're in position."

"Copy," Tanner's voice crackled back first. "So are we."

"Same here," Jackson replied.

"Gotta admit, can't see hide or hair of you," Asher said. "It's so dark out there we can barely see the house."

Peyton heard voices chuckle through the walkie-talkie. They ended the call and silence fell again. Minutes ticked by on her watch as they sat side by side, with Asher in the driver's seat, Peyton in the passenger seat and Spark stretched out in the back. She stared out at the night.

Half an hour passed. Then another. Until finally, around two thirty in the morning, Asher suddenly asked, "Have I done something that hurt you? You've been off for hours, and I feel like I should apologize for something again and I don't know what."

She'd been off? Did he not realize how moody he'd been?

"Why didn't you want me on this stakeout?" Peyton asked. "Why did you tell the chief you were worried about your ability to protect me? I shouldn't need to prove myself to you."

He lowered the binoculars and looked at her. She did too. And despite the darkness, she could see he seemed shocked.

"Of course I respect you," Asher said. "I told you that. You're so good at your job as a trainer that you intimidate me."

"Really?" Peyton felt her eyes widen. "I intimidate you?" Did Asher have any idea how intimidating he was? "I appreciate you saying that. Really, I do. But words aren't always enough. You out of anyone should know that."

She watched as his mouth moved like he was trying to get up the courage to say something but couldn't seem to form the words.

"If anything bad happened to you on this mission, I'd never forgive myself," he said.

Peyton reached across the front seat of the car and took his hand.

"Are you trying to prove to yourself, the chief or the team that you're able to protect me?" she asked.

He squeezed her hand for a long moment. Then he pulled back and so did she.

"Maybe all of the above," he said. "I'm worried the rest of the team thinks I'm a bad son for not wanting to see my father and a bad brother because Mara decided to go on the run instead of trusting me."

"I think if anybody is judging you it has more to do with what's going on inside them than with you," Peyton said. "Are you judging yourself?"

"What does it say about me that Mara won't listen to me?" Asher asked. "I've tried to convince her to turn herself in. Why won't she let me help her?" His voice rose like there was a pain deep inside him that was finally starting to bubble up to the surface. "What's wrong with me that my own sister won't trust me?"

*Lord, please guide my words right now. Help me know what to say.*

"We do know that she's very worried about you and your dad," Peyton said. "To the point that she's too afraid to do anything but hide. I think, anyway. She's making her own choices and that's not a reflection on you or your relationship. Ultimately, how she's handling things is not up to you."

Asher didn't say anything for a long moment, and instead he raised the binoculars to his eyes and stared down through the trees at the darkened house.

"You think I'm controlling?" he asked. He was still looking through the binoculars.

"I think you can be," Peyton said honestly. "But it's not who you are all the time and in every situation. I think you're comfortable leading, but I've also seen plenty of times you were happy to let other people take the lead. Why?"

"My ex-wife told me I was controlling, unlovable and paranoid."

Asher lowered his binoculars again but continued to stare out through the windshield into the night.

"When I met Lucie," he continued, "my exwife, and we started dating, she was finishing up her university degree. She was always incredibly busy with various projects and always stayed late into the night studying at the library. When our pastor was preparing us for marriage, he said it worried him that we lived pretty separate lives and that having really special date nights sometimes was no substitute for having day in and out quantity time together. But I figured her schedule would settle down once she graduated. After all, my career in law enforcement was incredibly busy and demanding too."

He paused and frowned. Peyton waited.

"She started her new job a week after we got married, and it was like her job became her whole life," he said. "She was on her phone constantly, even texting in bed at night, and was always disappearing on business trips. I began to suspect that she was having an affair with one of her male colleagues."

"I'm sorry," Peyton said. He glanced at her and smiled sadly.

"Then she got a new phone update and her phone automatically linked to our shared desktop computer," Asher said, "and her and her coworker's messages to each other started popping up on the screen. They were really inappropriate."

Peyton winced. She couldn't imagine how painful that must've been.

"I called her on it," Asher went on. "First she denied it, then she accused me of hacking her phone, and then when she realized what had happened she told me it was all a big misunderstanding and she wanted to stay married. We went to see our pastor together. She apologized to me, I forgave her and our pastor asked what I'd need to trust her again. I said no more business trips, no more late-night texts, and that I wanted complete access to all of her messages, emails and social media. Lucie exploded. She said I was paranoid and controlling, and that no woman in her right mind would ever love a man like me." Pain broke in his voice. "She left that day and moved in with him. They're married now."

"I'm so, so sorry," Peyton said again. The words seemed completely inadequate for what Asher was describing.

"The hardest part is that she made me out to be the villain," Asher said. "It's like between my ex-wife and my father's new family, I keep being painted as the bad guy, because of the stuff other people have done." He turned on the seat and faced Peyton. "What do you think about what I asked of her? Do you think I was wrong to ask all that? Or to expect that of any woman I wanted to be in a relationship with?"

As much as Peyton wanted to reassure Asher and take his pain away, she also wanted to be totally honest. He deserved nothing less.

"I don't know," she said. "I find it really hard to imagine ever being in her shoes. If you'd come to me back then as a friend and asked my opinion I would say that she had broken your trust and she needed to rebuild it. But that you should see this as step one of a process. Maybe no business trips for six months. No late-night calls for a while. Shared phone access within some parameters. But that checking up on her every day and monitoring her every move wasn't going to make you feel any safer, and it wasn't going to stop her from lying and sneaking around on you either. One day you still had to take a leap of faith and trust her—or whoever you decided to be with—and that's really hard to do."

A light flickered on below them at Gunther's house. Immediately both Peyton and Asher snapped their binoculars to their eyes. The first thing she saw was Gunther, through a small gap in the living room curtains. It looked like he was getting ready to go out.

Asher picked up the walkie-talkie.

"We've got motion," Asher said.

"Copy," Jackson said. "We've got visuals."

"Copy that," Tanner added.

The light switched off again. But a moment later, they saw Gunther walk out the front door with a large duffel bag over his shoulder. Motion sensor lights swept over the driveway, illuminating the scene. The narrow drive widened out at the end to make room for a black truck and a small white car. Gunther started for the truck.

The front door swung open again. Annika rushed out, in what looked like a long pajama top and bottoms, with a pink robe tied overtop.

"I've got Gunther," Jackson said.

"I'll keep eyes on Annika," Tanner confirmed.

They were too far away to make out the sound, but by the looks of things Annika was shouting at her husband and trying to stop him from leaving. Peyton glanced at her watch. It was 2:40 a.m.

"Either of you got audio?" Asher asked.

"Somewhat," Tanner said. "Lot of swearing. She's demanding to know where he's going this late at night."

"Good question," Asher said. "Let us know if he gives her an answer."

Annika grabbed at the bag. Gunther swung back and pushed her off of him.

"Nobody move in unless we have reason to believe her life is in danger," Asher said.

Peyton's fingers tensed into fists as she held the binoculars. Gunther's face was red as he shouted at his wife. Then he turned toward the truck. She ran for the white car, pressed a button on what he guessed was a key fob, and the car's engine turned to life. The message was clear: if Gunther drove off she was going after him.

Gunther yanked the door to his truck open.

"Guess we're going to have two vehicles to follow," Tanner said. "I'm going to suggest that we take Annika. Jackson, you take Gunther. Asher and Peyton will continue to watch the house."

Gunther grabbed something from inside the truck. He spun back and pointed it at his wife.

"It's a gun!" Tanner's voice filled the walkie-talkie. "Suspect has a gun!"

"Move in!"

But it was too late. Gunther aimed the gun at his wife's car and fired.

Asher watched through the binoculars as Annika's windshield shattered.

"Go, go, go!" Tanner yelled.

Asher threw the door open and leaped from the vehicle, as the sound of the gunshot and breaking glass still echoed in the air. In a second, Peyton and Spark were out of the car as well and by his side.

The K-9 officers and the recruits moved in, with their guns and badges drawn. Immediately, Jackson and his K-9 partner, Rex, converged on Gunther. He tried to run, but in moments they had him down on the ground in handcuffs. Tanner, his K-9, Britta, and the two female candidates ran for Annika. Asher breathed a sigh of relief as Annika walked away from her car. The windshield had caved in, and glass clung to her hair and clothes, but she otherwise seemed unhurt—just livid.

Within minutes they had secured the scene.

Jackson, Tanner, Parker and Brandie took Gunther and Annika into custody in two separate cars, while Owen and Veronica stayed behind to secure the house. Asher, Peyton and Spark drove down to join them.

"Unfortunately, the police won't be able to hold either Gunther or Annika for more than a few hours unless they press charges," Asher said, as they drove. "The fact Gunther fired his weapon at Annika definitely appears to be enough provocation to charge him with a crime. But according to Jackson, Gunther is already claiming that it was an accidental misfire and he was incredibly sorry. I don't know if Annika will want to press charges against Gunther, but it will be hard to make any charges for the gunshot stick if she doesn't, especially as it happened on their own property." He sighed. "It's hard to know what goes on in other people's marriages."

His mind flashed back to the moment Annika had gotten into the car to chase after Gunther. It had been years since he'd remembered the way his parents had fought in the days before his father left. His mother had later admitted to Asher that when it got really bad she used to try to follow him in her car to see where he was going, but that his dad would just drive around in circles, making her feel foolish. She also told him she felt relieved that his dad took Asher on sales calls, because she assumed he wouldn't cheat if his son was there. If his own amazing mother had been unable to keep her husband from cheating, what had made him think that he had the power to change what Lucie did?

"The good news is we've now got reason to search the house," Asher said. "Thankfully Tanner found out that neither of them own a gun license or any legally purchased guns. But again, no guarantee we'll be able to hold him for long, especially if he has a really good lawyer."

He frowned.

"It's a matchstick tower," Peyton said. "We just keep building."

"And it will eventually fall," Asher said.

But now the clock was ticking. Gunther was aware the police were watching him. There was no knowing what he'd do when he was released. If either Gunther or Annika had anything to do with the missing puppies, they'd be sure to move them as soon as they could.

Asher parked their vehicle in the trees, off the road and out of sight. Then the three of them walked down the long drive to join the two recruits in the front of the house. Together they searched the premises. Spark diligently sniffed around both the inside and outside of the house with Peyton and Asher in tow, while Owen and Veronica stayed in the driveway and watched for any sign of trouble.

But the search came up empty. No drugs, no guns and above all no bloodhound puppies. If Gunther and his wife were involved in criminal activity, they'd been smart enough to keep it outside their home.

It was after four o'clock in the morning when Asher rejoined the two candidates in the driveway, while Peyton took Spark for one final walk around the perimeter of the property. Thunder rumbled in the distance. The rain wasn't far off, and something in the air made Asher suspect that when it did arrive it would hit with a vengeance. Asher called Tanner, who said that he and Jackson were on their way back to pick up Veronica and Owen, so that Asher and Peyton wouldn't risk their cover by taking them back to the PNK9 training center.

Asher stood in the driveway, faced the pair and tried to stifle a yawn. Both of the candidates were dressed in blue jeans with PNK9 windbreakers and hats. Veronica looked every bit as tired as Asher felt. But Owen bounced on the balls of his feet with a broad smile and an almost nervous energy.

"Thanks for all your hard work," Asher told Veronica and Owen, "but we've hit a dead end and I think this is a bust. These kind of operations aren't easy, but you guys really brought your all and I'll be sure to put in a good word with the chief."

Asher heard footsteps and looked to see Peyton and Spark coming back around the building. Asher's and Peyton's eyes met. Her head shook and he sighed. If Peyton and Spark hadn't turned anything up then there was nothing there to be found.

*Lord, thank You for guiding us tonight.* Asher closed his eyes and prayed silently. *Please help us find and rescue the puppies before it's too late.*

Spark growled softly. He opened his eyes and looked at the dog. Spark's ears perked. His K-9 partner's tail began to swish. Spark had found something?

Peyton noticed it too. She glanced down at the dog. "Show me."

Spark raised his snout, sniffed the air and made a beeline for Veronica. The dog sat down at the trainee's feet and woofed confidently.

"Wow," Owen said. "I did not see that coming."

A panicked look crossed Veronica's eyes.

"What's going on, Veronica?" Asher asked, keeping his voice calm and level.

"I… I honestly don't know," Veronica said.

She sounded bewildered, confused and maybe even a little bit frightened. Asher reminded himself that it had been a very long night, all their adrenaline levels were high and nobody had gotten any sleep.

"Do you have anything on your person that you shouldn't?" Asher pressed.

"I don't," Veronica said. "I promise I don't."

Asher would've been tempted to believe her if Spark didn't seem so certain. He glanced to Peyton, who looked every bit as baffled and concerned as he felt.

"Well, I'm going to have to ask Peyton to pat you down," Asher said. "You're a law enforcement officer on an active case at a crime scene. We can't risk any evidence going missing. Even by accident." He added that last bit to be kind. "You can start by turning your pockets out and taking off your jacket."

Veronica nodded unsteadily, then pulled off

her jacket and passed it to Peyton. A small baggie fell out of the pocket and hit the ground with a muffled thud.

Peyton slid on a pair of gloves, bent down and picked it up. It was a green bud the size of a hazelnut. Asher recognized it even from a distance.

"Marijuana?" he asked Peyton.

"Certainly looks like it," she said. Peyton held up the bag and smelled it without opening it. It was one of the few drugs pungent enough a cop could smell it through plastic. "Smells like it too."

"I promise I've never seen that before in my life," Veronica said. "I wouldn't even know what to do with it."

Owen snorted. But again, as Asher searched her face he was certain she was telling the truth. But if his gut was saying one thing and the facts were saying the other, what he needed was more facts.

"When was the last time your jacket was out of your sight?" Peyton asked.

"I don't know," Veronica said. "I had it off in the car for a while."

Owen pulled a cell phone from his pocket, held it to his ear and started to walk down the winding driveway.

"Hey, Mom," Owen said loudly. "Wow,

you're calling late. Is everything okay with you and Dad?"

A second later, Owen had disappeared from view around a bend. Asher prayed and silently asked God for wisdom. There had been so many problems with the candidates—incidents that had interfered with the unit's cases. This was so much bigger than one bud of marijuana.

Asher turned to Spark. "Search."

Spark's ears perked and his snout rose. His partner woofed again, trotted over to Peyton and signaled to the baggie she was holding in her hand. The dog's shaggy eyebrows rose as if questioning why Asher would give him a task that simple.

Asher told Spark he'd done a good job and told him to look again. Spark sniffed the air. Asher held his breath. Then Spark started following in the direction Owen had gone. Asher felt a sinking feeling in the pit of his stomach.

He glanced at Peyton. "Search Veronica. Get any other details you can about what might be going on. Looks like I'm going to go have a chat with Owen."

Asher followed Spark down the winding driveway and then off a few feet into the woods. Owen's footsteps quickened as Spark drew closer, but even if the candidate had tried running, he would never have been able to outrun Spark. Asher could hear Owen still talking into his phone, but he couldn't see any light coming from the screen. Owen walked faster. Spark galloped after him, ran around in front of him and barked.

"Good dog," Asher said with a disappointed sigh.

Owen stopped walking. Irritation flashed across his face.

"Can you excuse me?" Owen said. "I'm on a very important phone call."

"Then you might want to check that they haven't hung up on you because your screen's gone to black," Asher said dryly.

He shone his flashlight toward the man, catching his entire form in its glow. Owen pocketed his phone and looked at Asher.

"Your dog's wrong," Owen said, almost smugly. "You're welcome to search me, but I don't have any drugs on me."

"As a K-9 officer, you should know that K-9s don't detect the drugs themselves, just the scent of them," Asher said, repeating what Peyton had taught him. Was Owen so arrogant he actually thought he could pull one over on Asher? "When you're dealing with something like marijuana in particular, the odor can linger for a few hours after someone's already ditched the drugs. Sometimes even days."

The confidence faltered in Owen's eyes. But the smile tightened.

"Either way, dog's wrong," Owen said.

No, Asher was pretty sure that Spark wasn't. Asher sighed. It was the early hours of the morning. He hadn't slept and he didn't have the energy for any kind of nonsense from Owen right now.

"I'm not going to argue with you," Asher said. "I'm just going to take both you and Veronica to headquarters, explain the situation to the chief and suggest he run a drug test on both of you."

Worry filled Owen's eyes. Then the candidate forced a chuckle.

"Come on, man," Owen said. "Don't be like that. You and I are on the same team."

"And what team is that?" Asher asked.

"We both want the best possible people joining the PNK9," Owen said. "You know as well as I do that it's ridiculous to have four candidates for two permanent spots, instead of just picking the most qualified person for the job. Now, Veronica already had an unfair advantage because she's Jasmin's sister, and now it turns out that Brandie is Nick Rossi's sister, and he's engaged to a PNK9 officer too. But you and I both know that when you're out there in the field, and up against some really big, bad guys, you want the very best of the best having your back. You can be honest with me. I saw how Donovan stuck you with Peyton instead of assigning you a real partner on this operation."

How could this man possibly think that Asher would be on his side? Peyton may not have had the same amount of field experience as Asher had. But she was a brilliant, meticulous and dedicated trainer who had a gut instinct that was second to none.

Asher couldn't tell how much of what was coming out of Owen's mouth right now was arrogance and how much was jealousy, but he didn't much care. He was tired. It was going to rain. And this man didn't deserve to wear a badge.

Plus, he had just disrespected Peyton.

What Asher needed to do right now was figure out exactly what Owen had done and get him to confess to it. But if he'd been Dan Johnson instead of Asher Gilmore, he'd have actually socked him one and called it a night.

Then it hit him. Right now, Asher could use Dan's help.

And just like that Asher felt the slow grin of the man who'd come to town looking to make friends with the wrong type of people cross his lips again. Asher's shoulders rolled back and he chuckled.

"Yeah, I know how it is," Asher said. He signaled Spark back to his side. "A team is only as strong as its weakest member, right? But some people just can't tell who's weak and who's strong. So sometimes you've got to give it a little push."

Like how Owen had pushed Brandie into traffic this summer?

"Right," Owen said and chuckled. "A push. You don't want Brandie, Veronica or even Parker getting a spot on the team. You want me."

"So, how do you make that happen?" Asher asked. "Hypothetically."

"Hypothetically?" Owen's grin grew wider. "It would be up to someone like us to point out the weaknesses in the system. For example, if I was able to plant a small baggie of weed into Veronica's pocket, that just goes to show that she doesn't have the situational awareness that you'd want for an officer in this unit."

Asher nodded. "I get it."

"Veronica should've been kicked from the team when her incompetence delayed her ability to aid in an active investigation months ago," Owen said. "Brandie let herself get nudged into traffic this summer, and Parker let himself get framed for it. Both of them should be automatically disqualified too."

"Because we don't want anyone in the unit who's weak enough to have something planted on them, or stolen from them, or be pushed, or get framed," Asher said.

"Exactly," Owen said. "It's just bad and sloppy police work. If, hypothetically, someone had been intentionally getting rid of the weak links on the team, that person would actually be doing you a major favor."

"Because I want the best person for the job," Asher said.

"And a strong team makes you look good," Owen said. "See, I knew you'd get it."

Owen's grin was so self-satisfied that Asher's skin felt slimy.

*Lord, I know my attitude hasn't always been the best over the past few months. But the fact someone like Owen thinks I'd go along with sabotaging the team for my own ego is a real wake-up call. Forgive me and help me change. And thank You that I'm finally seeing Owen's true colors.*

"So, what can I do for you?" Asher asked.

"First off," Owen said, "no drug test. Secondly, you go to the chief and explain to him that we can't have people like Brandie, Veronica or Parker on the team, for obvious reasons. Now, if Donovan still wants to add two new permanent members to the team, I don't care who gets the second spot, as long as I'm the clear winner."

"But what if he points out that you went off on a wild-goose chase a few months back because you got a dodgy text?" Asher asked. "Doesn't that prove someone can manipulate you?"

"Not if I sent it to myself so people would think Parker was the one sabotaging the team!" Owen said and laughed.

"I don't get it," Asher said. "I thought you were testing the team. You don't want people to know you were behind all that?"

"No, because they won't get it," Owen said. "They're not like you and me. You're cool. You get it. I sabotaged the other three candidates to make sure I landed one of the permanent spots on the team, but it's better that it's our little secret."

"And all that was just you single-handedly?" Asher asked. "No one else involved in the incidents you described?"

"Just me." Owen raised both hands proudly. "And that's why you want me."

There was the sound of footsteps crunching in the trees behind him. Asher turned to see Peyton standing there.

"I patted Veronica down and I didn't find anything," Peyton said. "She's sitting in the back of our truck. I've confiscated her phone and I've also called Donovan to alert him of the situation."

"Did you catch all of that?" Asher asked.

"Oh, I caught enough," Peyton said.

Yeah, Asher had heard more than enough too.

"Call him back and tell him that Owen just confessed to setting Veronica up," Asher said, "pushing Brandie into traffic and trying to frame Parker for it. Not to mention the incident with Veronica that started the series of sabotage."

Owen spluttered a string of swear words.

"Like I said," Asher told Owen, "I get it. You sabotaged the other candidates because you're convinced you're the best person for the team. What you missed is that what makes PNK9 strong is the fact we have each other's backs. For the record, Peyton Burns is one of the top K-9 trainers in the country. She's worth a hundred selfish twerps like you, and there's no one else I'd rather work alongside. So, either you surrender and I take you into custody, or you do something stupid and I'm forced to tackle you down to the ground." Asher pulled his gun from his holster and aimed it at Owen before he got any ideas. "Which one is it going to be?"

# TEN

Peyton watched as Owen grudgingly surrendered. The guy muttered rudely under his breath but didn't seem about to try openly challenging Asher. Tanner and Jackson showed up as they were walking Owen back to their vehicle, and Tanner took both Owen and an uncuffed Veronica back to PNK9 headquarters in Olympia to sort things out with the chief. Peyton didn't envy Donovan. She couldn't imagine how hard it would be for him to deal with Owen, knowing he'd given the candidate a shot on the team and all he'd done was hurt the PNK9 for his own ego.

Then Asher, Peyton and Spark returned to the lodge. They parked their vehicle in the same secluded lot near the marina and hurried back. The rain had begun to fall as they walked and was pouring down in sheets by the time they finally reached the lodge, soaking them both to the skin. They ducked under the closest awning and ran around the side of the building, skipping the front lobby to head back in through the same side door that Asher used when he took Spark out at night.

Every muscle in her body ached for sleep.

But as the trio reached the door, Peyton's eyes looked past it to where a figure was huddled on a bench against the wall. Her knees were pulled up to her chest and her head was buried in her hands.

"Ember?" Peyton called.

The young woman turned and looked at Peyton. Fear filled her gaze, tears streaked her cheeks and Peyton could see the telltale swelling of a fresh bruise underneath the girl's right eye.

Peyton sucked in a breath. She grabbed Asher's arm.

"Somebody hit her," she said quietly. "Give me a moment to talk to her alone, okay? But stay close."

The same crushing fatigue she was feeling filled Asher's face, but a fresh, protective anger flashed across his green eyes, and she could tell he wasn't about to sleep until he too knew that Ember was okay.

"You got it," Asher said. "Take Spark. He might help."

Silently Asher pressed the end of Spark's lead into Peyton's fingers. The warmth of his palm seemed to radiate up her tired limbs.

*Thank You, God, that I have a man like Asher who has my back. Please help me find the right thing to say to help Ember.*

Peyton hurried down the side of the building toward Ember.

"Are you okay?" she called. "What happened? Is there anything we can do to help?"

"I'm fine," Ember said without looking up.

Peyton sat down beside her on the bench. Spark leaned against Ember's legs and laid his head across her lap. His dark eyes looked up into her face under shaggy eyebrows. The springer spaniel whimpered softly, as if to let Ember know that he could tell she wasn't okay. Ember leaned down, wrapped her arms around Spark and buried her face in his fur. Spark licked her cheeks. And for a long moment Peyton sat there and watched the K-9 comfort Ember.

Then Ember pulled back and looked at Peyton.

"My boyfriend and I had a really big fight tonight," she said.

"Did he hit you?" Peyton asked.

Ember nodded.

"Is this the first time?" Peyton asked.

Ember paused. Then shook her head.

"He was really angry this time," Ember said. Fresh tears filled her eyes. "He wanted to borrow my lodge key card, the one that opens all the rooms, and I wouldn't give it to him. Laurence said his last girlfriend, who was also in housekeeping, let him borrow hers all the time. But apparently it stopped working today after the manager did some kind of reset on all the door locks."

Laurence?

Peyton's memory flashed back to the man in a waistcoat and gloves who'd helped Ember deliver their food the night before. Warning bells rang in the back of Peyton's mind. Had Laurence been using his ex-girlfriend's housekeeping key card to break into rooms and steal things?

She glanced back at Asher. He was standing up against the wall by the door, a few inches away from the pouring rain, and she could tell from the stern look on his face he'd caught what Ember had said.

Peyton took a deep breath, knowing she was about to take a major risk and hoping it would pay off.

"Ember," she said softly. "I didn't tell anybody this, but the man who broke into our hotel suite and stole stuff also attacked me. I was really scared of him."

Ember gasped. Her hand rose to her throat.

"Again, I didn't tell anyone," Peyton said. "Because I didn't want to make a big deal about it. But he grabbed me and hurt me pretty badly. And I didn't do anything to him. I was just there. I know you probably want to think that Laurence is a good guy and that he'll never hurt you again. But people like that need to be stopped before they hurt somebody else. Does Laurence have a tattoo on his wrist?"

Even without looking back, Peyton could tell Asher was holding his breath.

"Yeah," Ember said. "He made us get matching ones when we started dating, so everyone would know we were together. His cousin did it. Mine's on my ankle."

She crossed her leg toward Peyton and pulled down her sock. It was the same rough lines she'd seen on her masked attacker's wrist, and could now make out they were an *L* and an *E*, inside an uneven heart.

"I just want to go back home to my mom and dad's," Ember said. "They're in Portland. But Laurence said I can't quit my job here and that he'll be really mad if I go."

Peyton glanced at Asher. His steely gaze met hers.

*Do you trust me?* she asked him silently.

As if reading her mind, Asher nodded.

"Ember, I have a friend who's a police officer," Peyton started. Immediately, Ember started to shake her head. "But she's not at all like what you're probably thinking of right now. Her name is Willow. She's really kind and gentle, and she has a really cute German pointer named Star. Willow's actually going to have a baby really soon. She's a really nice person and you can trust her."

Ember relaxed slightly.

"If it's okay with you, I'm going to call her and ask if she can come help you," Peyton said. "She and her husband—he's really nice too—can help you get to your mom and dad's safely, and if you tell them what's been happening they can help make sure that Laurence never hurts anyone again. You can even keep it all anonymous if you want to. Nobody has to ever know you talked to the police."

Ember pressed her lips together. Peyton prayed.

Then Ember nodded. "Okay."

Peyton exhaled. *Thank You, God.*

She glanced back at Asher in time to see him dial PNK9 Officer Willow Bates's number and press the phone to his ear. He walked away down the lodge so they wouldn't overhear his call. She watched him go.

"Dan told me that he doesn't just think

you're pretty or whatever, he thinks you're really smart and respects you too," Ember said. "Which is part of why I stood up to Laurence when he wanted my card. I want somebody who's like your husband."

*Yeah, I do too.*

Peyton, Asher and Spark waited with Ember until Willow arrived in an unmarked car with Star curled up beside her on the front seat. Peyton, Asher and Ember sprinted through the rain toward them, with Asher holding his jacket over Ember's head to shield her from the rain. Ember gave Peyton a long hug, and Willow promised to keep her safe. Willow left with Ember. Asher and Peyton stood with Spark against the wall and watched them go.

"I talked to Donovan and they've issued an arrest warrant against Ember's boyfriend, Laurence," he said. "Based on what Ember told us about him, he sounds kind of slippery. So, it might not be easy to track him down and get him in cuffs. But at least we've finally figured out who our masked attacker is, thanks to you."

"And you," Peyton said.

"But it's not enough," Asher said. "Not by a long shot. He's still out there and we have no idea why he's after us. Until he's caught and locked behind bars, this won't be over. Even then, if he was sent by someone, they could still come after us another way. Our lives are still in danger and I'm not going to be able to rest until I'm sure we're safe. Until I know you're safe."

His voice caught in his throat and Peyton felt something tighten in her chest. The rain poured down like a sheet in front of them. She turned toward Asher. Wordlessly his arms parted, she slid in between them and Asher enveloped her in a hug. For a long moment, they stood there and held each other, just beyond the reach of the wind and the rain. She could feel Asher's heartbeat racing against her chest.

"I couldn't live with myself if I let something happen to you," Asher said. His voice was low and deep. "You're incredible. I know I'm not always the easiest guy to get along with. It really shook me that someone like Owen could think I'd ever place my own ego above the team. But please don't ever doubt how important you are to this operation and to me."

She tilted her face toward him. He was so close that she could feel his breath on her skin. His nose bumped against hers.

"I think you're amazing," she said. "The way you got Owen to confess like that was something else. You beat yourself up all the time and I don't even know why. You don't see how good at this you really are."

"Well, I think we make a pretty good team," Asher said.

He chuckled softly. It was a warm and affectionate sound.

"Me too."

"Then maybe we should team up more often."

His lips hovered over hers. For moment she thought that he was about to kiss her, and she was about to kiss him back, but instead he pulled away and took both of her hands in his. His mouth brushed her knuckles.

"You deserve better than a man like me," he said. "I'm still bread that's half-baked, and you should be with someone who's completely ready for you."

She wanted to tell him that he was wrong. But her mind filtered through everything he'd said back in the car. She loved her work—including the weekend training trips and long hours. Could she be with someone who'd always be worried when she was out of his sight? Would she be so focused on trying to help him overcome his pain and baggage that she'd lose focus on her own career?

He let go of her hands and stepped back.

"Can you take Spark upstairs and get him tucked into bed?" he asked.

"Absolutely."

"Try to get some sleep," Asher said. "Something tells me Donovan's going to want to wrap up this case soon and tomorrow could be a pretty long day."

She wanted to hold him close and take away the pain she could see brimming in his eyes. Instead, she took Spark's leash and watched as Asher pulled his hood over his head and walked off into the woods, with his shoulders slumped as if weighed down by his own doubts and fears.

Spark butted his head against Peyton's legs, and she ran her hand over the dog's silky ears. They went back in and walked down the hallway to their suite. She double-checked that nobody had been inside their rooms, then gave Spark some fresh food and pulled out the couch.

Even after changing into warm, dry clothes and curling up into her bed, she planned to stay awake and review case notes until she heard the click of Asher returning to the suite. Instead, she fell asleep within moments of her head hitting the pillow.

Peyton heard the sound of Asher knocking on the bedroom door and calling her name.

Her eyes opened to see sunshine streaming

through the cracks in the curtain and the clock saying it was almost noon.

"Hey," she called. "Thanks for waking me up." She stood up and pulled back the curtains, but didn't move to open the door. "I didn't realize it was so late."

"I am just glad you managed to get some sleep," Asher called back, and she wondered if he'd ever made it to bed or just spent hours walking in the rain. "I just got off a call with Donovan. Ember gave a full statement and her parents came to pick her up and move her home. A warrant was issued against her boyfriend, Laurence Deeks. Sadly, he's still in the wind. Owen squirmed his way to a confession and has been eliminated as a candidate for the PNK9. Donovan's in talks with the captain of the police department Owen works for, and criminal charges are being considered."

"Has anyone gotten a confession out of Gunther or Annika?" Peyton asked.

"Not yet," Asher said. "We have full team meeting in twenty minutes. I'm sure he'll fill us in then. I'm going to take Spark for a walk. Oh, and I got you some yogurt and things from the restaurant in the lobby."

"Thank you."

She got dressed and splashed some water on her face but waited until she heard Spark and Asher leave the suite before she opened the door and went into the main room. He'd folded the couch back up and tidied. There was fresh, piping-hot coffee, two containers of yogurt, and little plastic cups filled with different fruit, nuts and granola.

The rest of the team had already arrived on the video call when the suite door opened and Asher came back in with Spark. She smiled at him, he smiled back and then he picked up his laptop and logged in to the call from his usual seat on the far side of the couch, while Spark lay down in front of the fireplace. This time, along with Veronica, Tanner and Jasmin, they were joined by the entire PNK9 team, including Jackson, Willow, the other two candidates—Parker and Brandie—and officers Danica Stark, Colt Maxwell, Isaac McDane and Ruby Orton.

"I'm sorry to let you all know that Owen is no longer a part of the PNK9 recruit program and has been suspended from law enforcement," Donovan said, his face grave. "Thanks to Asher's excellent work the night before, we obtained a full confession for all of the incidents that have happened to Veronica, Brandie and Parker over the past few months. I'm sorry we didn't catch him sooner, but I'm glad we've now gotten this sorted and we can all move on with a clean slate. Let this be a reminder to all of us that the PNK9 is a team. There's no place for competitiveness, backstabbing or jealousy within our ranks. We are strongest when we work together and the most important thing I'm looking for in all new recruits who join the PNK9 is that they're a team player."

"Hear, hear," Isaac said.

"Well said," Jackson added.

"May I say something on that point before we continue?" Asher asked.

"Go ahead." The chief waved a hand.

"I just wanted to say I know I haven't been the easiest person to work with over the past few months," Asher began. "I've been moody and short. Even irritable. The situation with Mara has really been weighing on my heart, especially since my father is now involved. I know you all had a responsibility to keep an open mind about whether she's guilty or innocent, and I can't have made that easy on you. I just wanted to say I'm sorry and thank everyone for their patience." He glanced up over the laptop and looked at Peyton. "Especially you."

The group on the screen erupted in a chorus of officers all talking at once as they assured Asher that all was forgiven, they understood and he was a valued member of the team, until finally Donovan raised both hands palms up to call for silence.

"Thank you," Donovan said. "Let me assure you that everyone is committed to finding Mara, bringing her back safely and making sure she's treated fairly, regardless of how the facts in the case play out. In fact, we might've turned up a new lead in that investigation. When Port Angeles police raided Laurence Deeks's home in the early hours of the morning they found various items that had been stolen from the lodge over the past few months, including some of Stacey Stark's personal effects and her diary."

"Stacey had a small apartment at the lodge," Danica explained. She'd recently married Stacey's brother Luke and become stepmother to his baby son. "We think that Laurence broke in a few days after her death, while everyone was distracted, to see what he could steal. Luke's reading Stacey's diary now, and apparently there's a lot of negative stuff in there about her business partner, Eli Ballard. She was concerned he was involved in some criminal activity, and they'd fought about it."

"We'll be following up," Donovan said, "and seeing where it leads."

Peyton thanked God for the fresh lead. She

prayed it would bring Mara back soon and give Asher the peace that he needed.

"We have discovered the identities of two of the three crew members involved in the yacht smuggling incident last May, where water bottles filled with drugs went missing," Donovan went on. "Jasmin, can you pull them up?"

Jasmin nodded. Peyton heard the sound of typing, and then Vaughan's and Ridges's mug shots filled the screen.

"Vaughan Marks and Remus Ridge," Donovan said.

"Aka Vaughan and Ridges, the two thugs who sent us on that wild-goose chase two days ago and were following us around Rock River yesterday," Asher said.

Donovan's eyebrows rose. "Are you positive they're the same men?"

"One hundred percent," Peyton said.

"Well, that's encouraging," Donovan said. "Jasmin also managed to obtain some fuzzy security camera footage of the third member of the crew, the one that got put off the boat in Port Angeles before the Shiprider Law Enforcement Team moved in. Hopefully you'll be able to identify him."

"I suspect it's going to be Laurence," Asher said.

"Me too," said Peyton.

The screen clicked again. She glanced at the gray-and-white picture, expecting to see the man with the wrist tattoo who'd been threatening their lives.

Instead she blinked.

"That's Annika's son, Finn," she said.

Gunther's stepson, Finn, had been involved in smuggling drugs with Vaughan and Ridges, and then disappeared.

"Have we been able to get anything from Gunther and Annika?" Asher asked.

"They're still refusing to talk," Donovan said. "Both claim the gunshot was an accident. Gunther's lawyered up and is trying to get a judge to agree to his release. I'm going to package up everything we know about them, Laurence, Vaughan, Ridges, Finn and Gunther's Scuba Shop and pass it on to Shiprider for their ongoing investigation."

The feeling of dread began to drip down inside Peyton's core. She glanced at Asher and saw the concern she felt mirrored in his eyes.

"But what about us?" Peyton said. "What about our undercover mission to find the missing puppies?"

"Unfortunately," Donovan said, "I think the risks of continuing your undercover mission at this point outweigh the potential benefits.

While you two have done an excellent job untangling what looks to be a drug-smuggling case, we have no hard evidence that any of it connects to the three stolen bloodhounds."

"Except for the fact we have a witness who saw the dogs yesterday in the same model of boat that was purchased by Gunther's Scuba Shop and registered to Annika's son, Finn," Peyton said.

But even as she said it, she knew it wasn't enough. Donovan had already warned them he was considering pulling the plug on the whole operation. The danger kept growing, and while they'd identified the man who'd tried to kill them, he was still on the loose.

"Give us twenty-four hours," Asher said. "That's all I'm asking. Just one more day to wrap this up, before we give up on finding the puppies."

Donovan ran his hand over the back of his head. Peyton prayed.

"Okay," the chief said. "But I want to see a solid plan about what steps you're planning on taking next. And unless you come up with very compelling evidence that you're close to finding the dogs in the next twenty-four hours, this whole Dan and Merry undercover operation ends tomorrow."

* * *

As soon as the call ended, Asher dropped his laptop down on the couch and jumped to his feet. He looked over at Peyton. She stood too.

"We need a plan," he said. "Something solid and actionable that will help us find the puppies."

"Well," Peyton said. "What's your theory of the case?"

"Vaughan, Ridges and Finn tried to smuggle over a hundred thousand dollars' worth of cocaine in water bottles on some diplomatic dupe's yacht, last May," Asher said. He began to pace. Spark raised his head and watched him go. "Finn got caught doing drugs and left the boat. Law enforcement moved in. Ridges threw the drugs overboard. They now think the bottles are in some underwater caves."

"Why?" Peyton interrupted. "Why do they think the water bottles are in caves?"

"I don't know," Asher said. "Maybe because they floated away and never found them? Anyway, they heard that the PNK9 had been gifted three bloodhound pups who were being trained in narcotics detection and underwater skills. They stole the dogs, likely had them rush-trained by a professional who took a payout and now Finn has to be the one who has them out on his boat trying to sniff out the drugs."

"But if so why is Finn working with them?" she asked. "Why does his mother think he's gone missing? Why did they send us to smuggle a basically nothing package to Gunther? Why did Laurence try to kill us?"

He stopped and turned back. Her questions were irritating. But they were good too. Because he knew she was right. His theory had too many holes they still hadn't plugged.

He crossed his arms. "Okay, what's your best theory?"

"I'm wondering if Finn stole the bottles when he got off the boat," she said. "It could explain why he disappeared and why they can't find them."

Asher whistled. "Okay, that's smart. But then how do the underwater caves fit in?"

"I don't know," Peyton admitted. Her slender shoulders rose and fell. "Maybe we're wrong and it's not Finn."

When Jasmin had told them the person had been between five foot five and five foot eight, they'd theorized it could've been either Annika or Gunther. None of their other suspects were that short.

"But you know what else makes no sense?" Peyton added. "Why did Annika tell us to go check out Lake Crescent in Olympic National Park if we're interested in underwater caves? She even said it was her son Finn's favorite spot. But it's landlocked. We can't take *The Mixed Blessing* there. There's no way bottles dumped off a ship could've floated there."

"What if Annika suspects Finn stashed the drugs in an underwater cave there?" Asher said. "Maybe she thinks we're moving in on the local drug-smuggling trade, and she's so desperate to find him that she tipped us off?"

"But why would she betray her son like that?" Peyton said. "And if Finn did stash the drugs in an underwater cave in Olympic National Park, why would he need the PNK9's bloodhounds to find them now?"

"I don't know," Asher said. "But I want to go out there with Tanner and Britta. Spark can search for drugs, and we can get something with Laurence's scent on it so Britta will alert if our masked attacker makes an appearance." He ran a hand over his beard. Odd to think this might be his last day as Dan Johnson. "I'd like you to stay here, just to be safe. My mind's still on the fritz. I need to be focused and I don't want to risk your life if Laurence targets us again."

"Fine," Peyton said.

Fine? He'd expected her to argue with him.

Maybe, he'd even needed her to argue so that he could prove to both of them that he was right. "You're not going to fight me on this?"

"I'm tired of fighting you," Peyton said. Her head shook, sending her long red hair cascading out around her like flames. "I get that you're going through a lot. I respect that you're trying to handle it the best you can. You're the senior officer on this mission and if you think you have a better chance of finding our dogs if I stay behind, then I will."

He blinked. "But you think it's the wrong call."

"Yes, I think it's the wrong call." Peyton sat down on the couch. "But it's your call to make."

"I'm just trying to protect you," Asher said.

"It's not your job to protect me."

"Well, maybe I want it to be!" Asher's voice rose. Didn't she get that? Couldn't she see how much she mattered to him? "You know what hurts the most about the fact my father's memory is gone? It's that he'll never be able to tell me how many times he cheated on my mother and if it was with any of the women he introduced me to who I thought of as friends. I'll never know if maybe there's something I could've done to stop it. Something I could've seen. Something I could've told my mom or challenged him on."

Peyton looked up into his face.

"Asher, you were just a kid."

"But I wasn't when Mara went on the run," Asher said. "If I'd been there for her growing up, like a real big brother, maybe none of this would've happened. She might have come to me instead of running in the first place."

"Do you hate Ember for the fact her boyfriend nearly killed you?" Peyton asked. "Or me for not being there in the kennels when my assistant was attacked and the dogs were stolen?"

Asher felt his eyes widen. "No, of course not."

"Then stop blaming yourself for the mistakes everybody else made," Peyton said. She leaped to her feet and her voice rose. "You are lovable, Asher, and likable, and good at your job and worthy of respect. You just need to decide to start believing it. You're trapped in this prison of your own regrets and you're the only one who can set yourself free. But I'm done trying to argue with you. We've got less than a day to find those puppies. And whatever this is that's going on between us, I can't let it jeopardize that. So go, call Donovan and

Tanner, set up the dive, and we can talk more when you get back."

He stood there and stared at her for a long moment. Words he wished he knew how to say welled up inside him. But she was right. They didn't have time and he'd let his own baggage impact the PNK9 long enough. He swallowed hard. "Sounds good."

It didn't take much convincing to get Donovan to agree to the trip. This time, Tanner would bring the scuba gear, along with the trailer, boat and truck. Asher and Spark met him and Britta at the marina.

It took them forty minutes to get there, down twisting mountain roads that took them deeper and deeper into the park. Nestled in the northern end of Olympic National Park, Lake Crescent was a startling shade of blue and surrounded by huge towering mountains and thick, lush forest. The water was deep, cold and so crystal clear that scuba divers sometimes got in trouble by accidentally diving far deeper than they'd meant to. But apparently it made for beautiful diving with monstrous rocks, thick seaweed forests and small boat wrecks.

They boarded a small motorboat, where Tanner sat in the back with Britta and ran the engine, while Asher sat in the front with Spark.

The K-9s sniffed the air.

Tanner slowly navigated the small boat around the banana-shaped lake. There'd been an odd, aching feeling in the center of Asher's chest when he'd said goodbye to Peyton, and it seemed to be growing deeper every moment they were apart. He missed her. More than he'd ever imagined he could miss another person.

Why had he pushed her away? Yes, he'd been worried for her safety after what had happened last time they'd been diving. But had it been something more than that?

Spark barked sharply. The dog's commanding voice echoed over the lake.

Asher looked at his partner. "Are you sure?"

Spark woofed loudly and thumped his tail on the bottom of the boat.

"He sounds convinced," Tanner said.

"Agreed," Asher said. "Looks like I'm diving."

The lake water was both colder and deeper than diving off the coast of the Salish Sea had been the day before. Asher swam alone, leaving Tanner in the boat with the two dogs. He dove deep and scanned the rough and craggy rocks for any sign of a cave. Finally, Asher spotted it. There was a small gap in the rocks deep below him. He swam for it and pushed his way through. The tunnel was a tight squeeze, and he could feel his air tank scrape against the walls. The water was pitch-black in front of his eyes. But the channel was so narrow that he couldn't reach for a flashlight. His hands hit solid rock. He'd hit a dead end. Asher scrambled for a moment to get his bearings, wondering how he'd even begin to turn around. Then he felt empty space above him, swam upward, felt his head break through the surface of the water and climbed out into a cave.

Asher pulled off his mask and immediately smelled the scent of death. He switched on his flashlight. The light bounced off the rock. The cave was about the size of their living room back at the suite and only a few feet tall. A bag overflowing with plastic water bottles lay to his right, their contents spilling out onto the slippery rock. He crouched onto the balls of his feet and looked beyond it.

There lay a young man's body.

Asher's heart lurched as a picture of how the man had died began to form before his eyes.

He'd been dead for months. But despite the ravages of death, Asher could tell it was Annika's son, Finn. He'd managed to take off the top of his wet suit, showing his arms covered in nautical tattoos, and tried to wrap it around what Asher guessed was a devastating gunshot wound to his lower leg.

*Lord, have mercy on this man and those who loved him.*

Without even thinking, Asher reached for his phone and dialed.

"Hello?" Peyton's voice was faint and crackled.

"Peyton!"

"Hello? Asher? Where are you? The signal's so bad I can barely hear you."

It was only then that Asher's brain caught up with what he'd instinctually done. He'd called Peyton. Not Tanner who was near him in the boat. Or Donovan.

Faced with death, he'd called the one person whose voice he'd most needed to hear.

"I'm in a cave." His voice rose. "I found Finn and the drugs. He's dead."

He heard Peyton gasp a breath.

"I've only got a second," he said. "I've got to swim out of here, get back to Tanner and call it in. But it looks like you're right. When Finn left the yacht he stole the drugs and hid them in an underwater cave in Lake Crescent. I don't know if Vaughan and Ridges followed him here. But it looks like somebody shot him. He managed to make it into the cave to hide and bled out. CSI will be able to tell us more. But, it looks like he's been dead for months. Clearly we were wrong to assume he was the man in the sketch who'd been out on the boat with the dogs recently."

"Okay," Peyton said. "I'll fill the team in while you coordinate on the ground."

"Get somebody to pick you up and bring you out here," Asher said. "It would be good to have you here on the scene."

Where she belonged.

A muffled banging came through the phone. The sound was violent and relentless, as if someone was trying to break through wood.

"Are you okay?" he asked. No answer. "Peyton! Can you hear me? What's going on?"

"Hang on," she said. "I think someone's—"

Then he heard Peyton scream.

# ELEVEN

The menacing forms of Vaughan and Ridges seemed to fill the living area of the hotel suite. Fear washed over Peyton. She'd been in the bedroom pinning her blond wig back over her natural red hair when Asher had called. Then she'd heard banging from the other room and rushed in to find them there. One of them had slammed the suite door behind them, but she could tell at a glance the wood around the lock was splintered. With trembling hands, she put her phone on silent, slid her hand behind her back, tucked her phone into her back pocket and prayed that Asher would still be able to hear her and send help.

"Vaughan and Ridges," she said loudly. "How did you get in here? What are you doing here?"

"Mrs. Johnson," Vaughan boomed. "We need to talk to your husband!"

"Dan's not here," Peyton said.

Ridges strode to the bedroom door and flung it open.

"Yo, Dan!" Ridges shouted. "Come out, come out wherever you are!"

Vaughan stood over her, while Ridges searched the suite.

"My husband isn't here!" Peyton said. "Trust me, he wouldn't hide from the likes of you!"

"Tell me where he is!" Vaughan demanded.

"He went diving," Peyton said.

She prayed silently, hoping that Asher could hear that she was in trouble and that help was on its way.

"Tell me what you want from him," she said, "and I'll give him the message to contact you when he gets back."

She could hear her voice quaking. Okay, let them think she was terrified. Let them underestimate her. She was so much stronger than they knew. One way or another she was going to make it out alive.

"My boss has got a problem with your husband," Vaughan said. "That makes it your problem. Dan made a mistake and now he's got a debt to pay."

"Whatever this is, Dan's good for it." Peyton's chin rose. Merry was a woman who believed in her husband and knew he'd protect her. "You want him to do a job? Or run something for you? Fine. Get out of my suite and I'll tell him you stopped by."

Ridges strode from the bedroom to the kitchenette, then back to join Vaughan.

"He's not here," Ridges told Vaughan. "I say we send him a message."

Ridges reached toward Peyton's face, like he was about to touch her hair.

But his large paw had barely made contact before her hand shot up defensively and knocked his hand away.

"Get out!" she shouted.

Rage flashed in Ridges's eyes. His hands shot out and shoved her back hard. She fell into a chair. The cell phone fell from her back pocket. Pain shot through her limbs. She prayed the call hadn't ended.

Vaughan yanked a gun from under the back of his shirt and shoved it hard under Peyton's chin. The barrel of the gun dug painfully into her flesh.

"You are nothing to us," Vaughan said. "You get that? Your husband messed with our boss's business. That means now we've got to mess with him, until he makes it good."

"I don't know what you're talking about," Peyton said. She had to stall them. She had to buy time until rescue arrived. "What do you think my husband did to you?"

"The boss runs a tight ship," Ridges said, "and nobody's stupid enough to mess with it, or leak or let themselves get caught. Your husband seemed like a good man, so we gave him a chance to do some business with us—"

"You sent us on a wild-goose chase to deliver a whole lot of nothing!" Peyton said.

"Dan had to prove we could trust him," Ridges said. "Instead I hear that people have started getting arrested—"

"Who?" she asked.

Did they mean Gunther? Annika? Had the police found Laurence?

The gun pressed deeper into her skin.

"I don't know if your husband said something stupid to someone on purpose or by accident." Vaughan leaned so close she could feel his hot breath on her face. "Maybe he has some past problem with a cop and they trailed him here. I don't know. We don't care. We don't tolerate mistakes or failure. So, now we gotta send a pretty strong message for him to find when he gets back, that when mistakes happen somebody's gotta pay."

She heard the clink of the safety being switched off the gun. He was going to kill her and leave her body here for Asher to find.

Panic welled up inside her. Terrified tears filled her eyes,

*Help me, Lord. What do I do? What do I say? How do I convince them to let me out alive?*

Suddenly she knew.

"I know about the bloodhound puppies!" she yelled.

The gun fell from her skin. Both Vaughan and Ridges stepped back. They looked angry and confused.

Vaughan swore. "What did you say?"

"I lied," Peyton said. "I know everything. I know that you two tried to smuggle some cocaine in water bottles on a yacht. I know some guy called Finn double-crossed you, stole the drugs and stashed them somewhere, so you stole some police dogs because you thought you could train them to find them."

Vaughan's eyes bulged.

"How could you possibly know that?" Vaughan demanded.

"Because I know somebody who knows someone in the Coast Guard," Peyton said. "So, we came here, we played you and we tried to gain your trust because we wanted in."

It was a risk. A huge risk. But one that just might keep her alive.

"I say we kill her," Ridges said to Vaughan. "We don't need this right now."

"If you kill me you'll never find those drugs," Peyton said. "You willing to risk a one-hundred-and-twenty-thousand-dollar stash? I'm a dog trainer! I've trained dogs to attack, and I've trained them to fight. You make me your partner. You take me to those dogs, and I promise you that I'll find you those drugs. On my life."

A pause stretched out between the two men that seemed to last an eternity.

Then Vaughan leaned toward her.

"You better hope you're not bluffing," he said, "because there are worse ways to die than a bullet to the brain."

Suddenly, strong hands grabbed her body and pulled her down to the floor. She felt something wet and sickly sweet clamped over her mouth. Dizziness swept over her. A deep and heavy unconsciousness pulled her under. She could feel something thick wrapping around her body. Then she was lifted, carried down a flight of stairs and tossed into a vehicle. Darkness filled her eyes. Desperate prayers to God filled her heart.

Asher would find her. He'd rescue her.

She had no idea how long she floated in and out of consciousness in a drugged-out haze, until slowly she became aware that she was seated again. Her hands were tied to the arms of a wooden chair. A gag filled her mouth. The smell of damp and musty air filled her nostrils. Then she heard whimpering.

Slowly her eyes adjusted to the darkness. She was in a cellar of some kind. Something was moving in the corner of the room. There were three bloodhound dogs, a little over a year old, underfed and matted but alive. Tears sprung to her eyes.

It was Agent, Chief and Ranger.

She'd finally found them.

"Where is she?" Asher called as he ran down the lodge's hallway, with Spark at his heels, to where law enforcement officers and hotel staff crowded around the open door to their suite. Yellow police tape crisscrossed the doorway.

He'd left Tanner and Britta back at Lake Crescent to coordinate the recovery of Finn's body and the drugs with emergency response, unhitched the trailer and driven back as quickly as he safely could. Still, it had been over an hour and a half since he'd heard Vaughan and Ridges break into the suite. Helplessly, Asher had listened as the two thugs had demanded to see him and then ominously threatened to "send him a message." Then there'd been a crash and the call with Peyton had disconnected. Despite countless calls to Donovan and the other members of the team, Peyton still hadn't been found.

As he drew near, he saw the acting operations manager, Ray Skerritt, about to get in his face with pathetic excuses about how nothing like this had ever happened, and a local police officer about to tell him the crime scene was closed.

But then Jackson lifted the police tape, stepped in front of the others with his K-9 partner, Rex, by his side and ushered Asher inside the suite.

"Please, tell me we've found her," Asher said.

Jackson shook his head.

"Not yet," he said. Jackson's eyes were grave. "Let's go out to the balcony. Where we can talk in private."

Jackson led Asher through the room that just hours earlier had felt like his and Peyton's cozy home base. Rex and Spark trotted behind them. The suite was filled with crime scene investigators, PNK9 officers and local police combing over every square inch of the suite. A chair lay turned over on its side. The leaf-patterned carpet was missing. They walked out onto the balcony with their K-9 partners and Jackson closed the door behind them.

Jackson turned to face him, and Asher was oddly thankful that whatever came next, Jackson wasn't the kind of officer to either drag it out or sugarcoat it.

"It appears Laurence disabled the back door security camera," Jackson said. "Staff caught him on video, but sadly didn't call police. It seemed Vaughan and Ridges came up the stairs. They used a key card that Laurence had stolen from the locker room to unlock the door and a small chisel and body weight to break the dead bolt. We estimate they were here with Peyton for a little under ten minutes before leaving and taking her with them. The green delivery van was seen pulling around the side of the building about five minutes before you called Peyton and leaving about fifteen minutes later."

Asher's breathing had gone shallow. He forced himself to gasp a long and deep breath.

"Here's where we're at in the investigation," Jackson continued slowly. "CSI is processing the scene. Law enforcement across the state are on the lookout for the van. Unfortunately her phone was left here, so Jasmin's unable to trace it. We're doing everything we can do."

But there had to be more, Asher thought. There had to be a way to find Peyton. Then he heard Jackson take in a deep breath.

"Also," Jackson went on, through gritted teeth, "we've got some bad news about Gunther. His lawyer got a judge to agree to a hearing and Gunther was released twenty minutes ago. Personally, I suspect some underhanded dealing went on there, but who knows. Law enforcement tailed Gunther and lost sight of him in Puget Sound. Apparently, he had a hidden boat waiting."

Asher turned toward him.

"I need a helicopter," he said, "and a team. I'm going to go find her."

Jackson raised his hands, palms up.

"We've already got the Coast Guard, park rangers and state troopers searching for her, by air, land and sea," he said. "The chief is on his way. He's just coordinating with Tanner and the body recovery team. Donovan will pick Tanner up and they'll be on their way here by helicopter. For now, you just hold tight and pray."

Jackson's phone began to ring. He pulled it out and glanced at the screen.

"One minute," Jackson said. "I've got to take this." He turned to go. Then he paused and laid a comforting hand on Asher's shoulder. "It's going to be okay. We're going to get her back."

Jackson went back into the suite with Rex, leaving Asher alone on the balcony with Spark.

Asher turned away from the door and toward the trees. He grabbed ahold of the railing with both hands and clutched it tightly. Spark whimpered softly and leaned up against his leg. His heart ached so much, it hurt with every beat.

*Help me, Lord, I feel helpless...*

It was like helplessness was an invisible enemy that he'd been trying to evade for as long as he could remember. For years he'd clung to the belief that he was somehow the one to blame—that he could've stopped his parents' marriage from ending, his wife from cheating and Mara from being on the run—because it was easier to hate himself than face the fact some things were beyond his control.

But now, Peyton was in danger, he didn't know how to find her and he hadn't been able to protect her.

He let go of the railing and let his hands drop. He felt the soft and gentle warmth of Spark nuzzling his hand. Asher ran his hand over the back of the dog's head.

"I wish I could promise you that nobody will hurt Peyton and everything will be okay," Asher told him. "But I can't." Unshed tears choked in his throat. "But I promise you that I'll never stop looking for her and trying to bring those who took her to justice."

He heard the sliding door open and turned. It was Jackson with Rex.

"Okay, I've got a small bit of positive news," Jackson said. "Local police have apprehended Laurence. He apparently came here looking for his girlfriend, Ember, and then was hiding out in the lodge. A colleague turned him in. Local police picked him up. They've got him sitting in an empty conference room downstairs. Chief's still en route, but he wondered if you wanted to question Laurence before they took him in."

Asher took a very deep breath and silently prayed for wisdom.

Peyton's life depended on Laurence telling them the truth. And they were running out of time. If Lawrence refused to talk to police or demanded a lawyer, Peyton could die.

"My cover hasn't been blown yet, right?" Asher said. "As far as Laurence knows, I'm still Dan Johnson and it's my wife, Merry, that's missing?"

"We've kept the circle of information very tight so far," Jackson said. "Need to know only. I'd say your cover is still secure, but it's hanging on by a pretty thin thread."

"Fair enough," Asher said.

Hopefully it would hold up for one final mission.

"I'm going to try to run a play on him," Asher said. "But that will require him thinking that I'm Dan and that I'm not working with police. So, we'll need to get local police to let him go. I'll call you once I'm in position, then you get them to release him."

He held his breath, knowing what a big risk he was taking by asking the cops to release him. If Asher's undercover play failed, they could lose their only lead.

Jackson didn't even blink. "Okay," he said. "Your play, your call."

Asher smiled and thanked God for his team.

"Thanks," Asher said. "Just make sure he goes out the side door."

"Will do."

Asher strolled back through the suite with his K-9 partner by his side. They jogged down the staircase and along the wall to the side parking lot. Then he called Jackson and let him know he was in position. Asher waited and prayed.

Spark began to growl.

"Show me," Asher said.

Sparks sprinted down the side of the building with his human partner one step behind him. A tall figure in an oversize coat slipped out from the side door and made a beeline for the trees. Asher rushed at him, grabbed him by the back of his jacket and spun him around. Laurence reached for his pocket and yanked out a knife. He swung. The blade flashed in his hand. But before he could strike, Asher blocked the blow, grabbed him by both arms and pushed him up against the wall so forcefully the knife fell from the man's hands. Asher looked down at the tattoo on his wrist then up into the man's bloodshot eyes.

"Not so tough without a gun or a knife, are you?" Asher asked. "Now, where's my wife?"

"I don't know!" Laurence shouted and swore at him.

Spark snarled and bared his teeth. The hackles on the back of Spark's neck rose. This time Asher didn't call him off.

"You're lying," Asher said. "You tried to shoot us, you tried to stab us and you broke into our suite. Now my wife is missing and you're the prime suspect. So be happy all I'm asking for are answers."

Laurence's face paled.

"I didn't hurt her," Laurence said.

Asher pushed him firmer against the wall. "You tried to."

"That wasn't personal," Laurence said. "I told Gunther I wanted to work for him. He said I was too small potatoes and that he didn't trust me, but that if I found the bottles he'd give me a cut. Then you showed up with a boat and I had to scare you off."

"Or kill off the competition," Asher said. "Now tell me where Vaughan and Ridges would take Merry and I'll let you live."

Relief flickered across Laurence's eyes like the kid in a spelling bee who'd just been asked to spell a word he knew.

"Gunther has a cottage," he said. "It's big. Like really expensive big. On the coast where the other big houses are. But it's not very nice because there's no furniture or anything. We always go there by boat. But he blindfolds me so I don't know how to find it."

"Nice try," Asher said. "Gunther doesn't have a third property. Just the house and the store."

"His name isn't on it," Laurence said quickly. "He got it from someone who owed him money. Robert something. I think maybe Bob or Bobby. I don't know." He was sweating now, like a guy in a standoff who'd just run out of ammo. "Please, you gotta believe me and that's all I know."

Asher searched the man's face. Yeah, he believed him that that was all he knew about Gunther's cottage. As for anything else about his criminal endeavors, he was sure the police interrogation would wring it out of him.

He stepped back and let him go.

"Okay, I believe you."

"So, we're all good?" Laurence asked.

Asher chuckled. "Not even close."

He yanked his badge from his pocket and held it up in front of Laurence's eyes for a fraction of a second. Laurence's face went white. Asher spun the man around and pinned him back against the wall. "My name is Officer Asher Gilmore of the Pacific Northwest K-9 Unit. This is my partner, Spark, and you are under arrest."

# TWELVE

Peyton had no idea how long she'd been in a dark room, tied to a chair and battling the dizziness left as whatever they'd drugged her with began to wear off. But every time she felt sleep threatening to drag her down again, the sound of scuffling and whining coming from the corner of the room made her grit her teeth and force herself to wake up.

The bloodhound puppies were here.

Ranger, Agent and Chief needed her to stay strong and to stay alive.

She seemed to be in some kind of basement. Faint light trickled in through two dingy and rectangular windows just below the ceiling. The floor was cracked concrete and the walls were brick. If she craned her head, she could barely make out several large and unplugged chest freezers set against the wall behind her, and she wondered if there were drugs or weapons inside. A single metal door was set in the wall opposite her. There was no door handle on her side, just a piece of metal welded over the place one would've been.

The dogs cowered in the corner of the room as if frightened to come out of the shadows. She tried calling out to the dogs through her gag. But her voice was so muffled and faint she couldn't sound out their names. Would they even remember their names after all these weeks? Or any of their training? Her hands were tied to the arms of the chair at her wrists, but her palms and fingers were free. She kept calling to them, trying to slowly sound out their names and reminding them that they were good boys, the best she could. She began to signal them too, using the hand signals she'd taught them, and tapped her fingers on the wood, mimicking the sound of her K-9 training clicker. The dog's ears perked toward the sounds.

*Good boy, Chief. Good boy, Agent. Good boy, Ranger. Come. Come.*

Slowly the bloodhounds' heads began to turn. She didn't know what the dogs had been through or what would happen to them next. But she needed them to know that someone cared about them.

Tentatively the dogs crept out of the corner

of the room and took a few tentative steps toward her. Their tails were tucked between their legs, their eyes were glassy, and their beautiful black and tan fur was matted and streaked with mud. And yet as she patiently called and coaxed them, she watched as their heads rose hopefully toward her, as if beginning to remember who she was and that she was safe.

Ranger was the first one to cross the floor toward her. His tail stayed down and his shoulders were hunched, as he inched toward her, staying as low to the ground as possible. A low growl rumbled in his throat.

*Good boy, Ranger. Come.*

She kept calling to him, gently and patiently, as he crawled toward her, until finally he sniffed around her feet. Then, tentatively, Ranger licked her fingers. Then his tail wagged. He barked and leaped up, pressing his paws against her knees. Grateful tears filled Peyton's eyes. She twisted her hands around inside her bonds and ran her fingers over his ears as best as she could.

*Yes, it's me. I won't hurt you. You're safe. You're loved.*

Ranger ran back to the corner of the room and sniffed around Agent and Chief. Then he came back with the other two behind him. Agent was limping slightly, putting tentative pressure on his front right paw. It looked sprained but not broken. The three bloodhounds surrounded her, sniffing her, bumping their heads against her legs, licking her, leaping up and nuzzling their heads into her lap. They remembered her. She stroked them back the best she could, running her fingers over their heads and making soothing and comforting sounds through her gag.

*Thank You, Lord. Please help me find a way to protect them, keep them safe and get them out alive.*

Finally, the dogs seemed to tire themselves out and curled up on the floor, pressing their bodies up against her legs and resting their paws and heads on her feet.

Then she heard a smattering of footsteps. There was someone in the room above her.

"Peyton!" Asher's voice sounded faintly. He was shouting her name. "Peyton! Are you here?"

*Asher! I'm here!*

She shouted his name as best she could through the gag, but all she could manage was a muffled cry. She rocked her chair back and forth, trying to make the legs clatter and bang on the cement floor.

But she could tell by the way he was shouting her name that he couldn't hear her.

Asher didn't know she was there.

"Britta's lost the scent in the middle of the room!" a second voice shouted. It was Tanner. "I don't think she's here!"

*I'm here! Below you!*

The dogs' ears perked and their heads rose toward the sound.

"Speak!" Peyton commanded the dogs. "Speak!"

She signaled the dogs with hand gestures and tapping, and shouted through her gag as loudly as she could.

The dogs began to yip and bark.

*Good boy! Speak! Louder!*

Then the dogs began to howl. Their deep, rich and mournful voices echoed off the walls and reverberated through the room.

"I hear them!" Asher yelled. "It's the bloodhounds! And Peyton!"

"I hear them too!" Tanner called.

"Peyton!" Asher shouted. "We're here! Hold on! Keep them going! We're coming! We just need to find a way into the basement!"

Suddenly the metal door flew open. A man stepped into the room. It was Ridges.

The puppies began to snarl and bark. They pressed themselves closer to Peyton. She could feel the puppies trembling in fear.

Ridges yanked a gun and aimed it at her.

"You make those dogs settle down and shut up!" Ridges shouted. "Or I will kill them and you!"

The need to find Peyton and the puppies surged through Asher's veins like adrenaline. The mournful howls beneath his feet had changed to angry barks and snarls. He and Tanner shouted her name, as they ran from room to room inside the large and vacant cottage, with Britta and Spark by their side. They threw open door after door, desperately trying to find a flight of stairs that would lead them down to the basement. But all they found were empty rooms.

It hadn't taken long for Jasmin to cross-reference large, expensive coastal houses against people with a name like Bob or Robert who had a criminal history or were likely to owe money to the wrong kind of people. They'd narrowed in on an area where neighbors had complained about hearing howling. They'd taken *The Mixed Blessing*, with Britta in the bow sniffing the air for Peyton's scent. Britta had found it, and they'd traced the scent to this large and empty house, before losing it in the middle of the kitchen.

Clearly, they'd found the right place and Peyton was somewhere below them, but they couldn't find a door leading downstairs. There had to be another way down. Desperately Tanner led Britta from room to room, hoping she'd recatch the scent. Suddenly, Britta barked at a door. Tanner burst through, with Asher and Spark one step behind him, and the K-9 officers found themselves back outside again. The sun was just beginning to set. A cold wind swept the air. The boxer led them down the side of the cottage. Then Asher spotted what looked like a cellar door, half-buried under a camouflaged tarp at the other end of the wall. Britta started to lead them toward it.

A burst of gunfire sounded from the tree line.

Asher and Tanner dropped to the ground behind a low garden wall and summoned their K-9 partners. Bullets whizzed past them, hitting the wall and sending splinters flying. Asher waited for a gap in the gunfire, crouched up and glimpsed who was firing from the trees. He dropped back down.

"It's Vaughan," Asher told Tanner.

Tanner glanced over the wall.

"I only see one gunman," Tanner said.

"Same here," Asher said.

Tanner glanced back down the wall to the door they'd exited through.

"I'll cover you," Tanner said. "I can make it back to the door and then draw his fire."

"You sure?" Asher asked.

Tanner nodded resolutely. "Absolutely."

But Tanner was a good man and a terrific PNK9 officer. What if Tanner got shot trying to protect him? Asher had to trust his team.

"Thanks," Asher said. "See you on the other side."

He held his breath, waited, and watched as Tanner and Britta made their way back down the wall toward the kitchen door, while Vaughan fired toward them. They slipped inside the kitchen door. He watched as Tanner raised his weapon at the ready and waited for Vaughan to fire again. Then the second Tanner heard the bullet ricochet against the wall, the PNK9 officer leaned around the doorframe and fired. Vaughan shouted out in pain, and Asher knew that Tanner's precise shot had hit its mark.

"Go!" Tanner shouted. "I got this!"

Fresh gratitude swelled in Asher's heart. He signaled Spark and they ran down the side of the house, away from the gunfire and toward the cellar door. Behind him he could hear Tanner and a wounded Vaughan exchanging gunfire. Asher reached the edge of the house, and then he and Spark sprinted across the open ground. He pulled the tarp back and looked down to see a metal door set deep in the ground. Spark sniffed the air. He woofed loudly. There were drugs down there and Spark could smell them.

Asher yanked the door open. A dank and narrow staircase lay ahead of him.

"Show me."

Spark barked and ran down the stairs with Asher at his heels.

He could hear the sound of the bloodhound puppies barking. He was nearing the bottom of the stairs when he heard a gunshot sounding through the hallways below him.

His heart leaped into his throat.

Had Peyton been shot? Had Spark?

A figure appeared at the bottom of the stairs. It was Ridges. He startled as if he hadn't expected to see Asher there. Ridges raised his gun and aimed at Asher. But Asher wasn't about to give him time to fire. He leaped at Ridges, knocking the gun from his hand and sending both men tumbling down to the bottom of the stairs. Asher landed on top, pinned Ridges against the ground and knocked the air from his lungs.

"Where is she?" Asher crouched over him. "Where. Is. My. Wife?"

"You're too late!" Ridges said. "She's gone!"

Nah, Asher wasn't about to believe a word coming from this vile man. Asher flipped him over, pulled a pair of zip tie handcuffs from his pocket and cuffed his wrists together. He hauled Ridges up to the top of the stairs and out into the trees. Tanner and Britta were running toward him.

"One down!" Tanner shouted.

"Got a second one for you!" Asher called back.

"Got it!" Tanner said. "Backup is on its way. You're good! Go!"

Asher pushed Ridges against the ground and ran back down the stairs. He couldn't see Spark anywhere. If the dog had found drugs, Spark knew to come back and get Asher. Where had his partner gone?

Asher ran from one empty room to another. He could hear Spark barking and the puppies howling. But he couldn't see them anywhere. He followed the sound of Spark's frantic barks into an empty room at the end of the hall. He'd reached the end of the basement and there was nothing there. What looked like a plywood wall lay ahead of him. For moment he wondered if he'd hit yet another dead end.

"Spark!" he shouted. "Where are you?"

His K-9 partner howled from behind the wood. Whether Asher could see it or not, he knew there had to be a hidden door. He threw himself against the plywood and burst through the unseen door into a concrete room.

There in the dim light sat Peyton. She was bound and gagged. But her face rose and her eyes met his, clear and unflinching. Agent, Ranger, Chief and Spark stood around her like a protective shield. His partner woofed triumphantly. Hot and grateful tears pushed to the back of his eyes. "Good job, Spark."

He looked down at Agent, Ranger and Chief. The dogs watched him warily. But they parted to let him through. Asher ran for Peyton and pulled the gag from her mouth.

"Are you okay?" he asked. He quickly cut the ties binding her hands. "Are you hurt?"

"I'm okay," Peyton said. "Just a little sore."

"Does this room have any other entrances or exits?" he asked.

She shook her head. "No. Just that door."

Which he might never have found without his K-9 partner's help.

"How are the dogs?" he asked.

"Bit worse for wear," she said. "But they'll be okay."

He brushed his hand along her cheek. "I heard a gunshot."

"Ridges tried to shoot me," she said. "But first the puppies got in his way and wouldn't let him get anywhere close to me. Then Spark burst through and startled him just as he was about to fire, so he missed and hit the wall. He slammed the door and ran, leaving Spark locked in here with us."

She stood on shaky legs. He gathered her up to his chest and hugged her as if she might break. But her arms clamped around him strong and tight.

"I'm so sorry it took so long to find you," he said, feeling the words catch in his throat.

"I never doubted you would." Her lips brushed in a fleeting kiss across his cheek.

Spark ran around behind Peyton and barked. It was only then Asher noticed the half dozen unplugged freezers that lined the walls.

"I suspect Spark's found the mother lode," Peyton added.

Together they walked over to the freezers. The bloodhounds followed, sticking close to Peyton's side. He flipped the closest freezer open. Bricks of white powder were stacked inside. The one beside it contained guns.

"Backup is on their way," he said. "There will be a lot for law enforcement to process. But for now, let's get you and the puppies out of here."

Asher led Peyton through the labyrinth of tunnels back to the stairs. The four dogs followed them closely. They ran up the stairs and back into the evening air. The sun was slipping deeper in the sky. The air had gotten colder. Asher looked to see Tanner and Britta off to his right standing over Vaughan and Ridges, guarding them both, as Peyton's kidnappers lay bound on the ground.

As Tanner laid eyes on Peyton, his face burst into a smile.

"Sure is good to see you!" he called.

"Good to see you too," she said. "Thanks for all your help."

"Anytime," Tanner said. "Got through to the chief. Backup is about ten minutes out."

Peyton turned to Asher. "Is there somewhere warm and quiet we can take the dogs? It's chilly, and soon there will be a whole lot of people arriving. They've been through a lot and I don't want them getting scared by the lights and noise."

"*The Mixed Blessing* is docked at the waterfront," Asher said.

"Let's go."

They hurried through the trees down an overgrown path that led to the coast, with Spark and the bloodhound puppies at their heels. The property had a large private beach and a long H-shaped dock, both of which looked like they'd once been lavish but had clearly been neglected. *The Mixed Blessing* sat docked at the very end, with the deep blue water of the Salish Sea spreading out behind it all the way to the green coast of British Columbia in the distance.

Peyton ushered the dogs onto the boat then climbed on after them. Peyton and Asher went below deck into the small cabin. Spark followed them down. Peyton called for Agent, Ranger and Chief. But the three bloodhounds crowded around the doorway. Their tails wagged anxiously. Peyton sat on the bench seat just inside the cabin and looked up at the three pups, as they danced around the top of the stairs.

"I think they're nervous about going down the stairs," Peyton said sadly. "Which makes sense if they've been kept in a basement."

"Hey, it's okay," Asher said. He sat down beside her. The boat rocked and swayed as if knocked by a wave. "You're an excellent trainer. You'll remind them who they are. After all, they remembered you, and you helped me remember who I want to be."

She turned toward him. His eyes searched her beautiful face, as words he didn't know how he'd ever find the courage to say filled his heart. He wanted to tell her that he wasn't ready for their adventure together to end. He wanted to set sail with her again and go diving. He wanted to sit by the fire at night and talk about their hopes and their fears. Asher felt like he was standing on the edge of a very high diving board looking down into cold water below, trying to get up the courage to jump.

He reached for her hand, and she let him take it in hers.

"I missed you today," he said. "More than I ever knew was possible. I was wrong to ask you to stay behind at the lodge. Not because of what happened with Vaughan and Ridges. And not only because you're a talented member of the PNK9 and any mission is better with you—although that is also true. But because I'm better when I'm with you."

The boat rocked again, harder this time. The bloodhounds began to whimper. Peyton pulled away, stood up and looked out. "We've drifted away from the shore!"

She started up the steps and he followed. The boat rocked beneath them. The pungent smell of gasoline filled the air. Peyton gasped in fear. A moment later Asher reached the deck and saw why.

Gunther stood in the front of the boat, with a metal gas canister in one hand and a flare gun in the other. A few final drops of amber liquid dripped from the can into the pool at his feet. The boat had been untied and was drifting away from the shore. An evil grin crossed Gunther's face. The barrel of his weapon swung back and forth from pointing at the pool of gasoline at his feet to the center of Peyton's core, as if he couldn't decide whether to just murder her or explode the boat and kill them all. The bloodhound puppies cowered.

"I warned you I don't like people who try to mess with my business," Gunther said. "Now you're going to tell me exactly what I need to know or I'll kill you here and now."

# THIRTEEN

Peyton felt Agent, Chief and Ranger press up against her legs. They were trembling in fear. Asher stepped in front of Peyton and the dogs like a protective shield, with Spark by his side. She reached down, brushed her fingertips over the bloodhounds' heads and tried to reassure them it was going to be okay.

"Don't be a fool," Asher said. "Vaughan, Ridges and Laurence were apprehended by police. Law enforcement are on their way to confiscate whatever stash of drugs and weapons you have in this place. There's nothing left. It's over."

"Do you think I care about any of that?" Gunther snapped. But Peyton could see full well in the man's eyes he did. He was angry. More than that, he was rattled. "Laurence was a liability and a loose cannon. I didn't even trust him enough to let him carry for me.

Vaughan and Ridges let Finn steal my merchandise from a yacht and then couldn't find it."

"Did you shoot him?" Asher asked. "Did you kill your own wife's son?"

"So you found Finn's body," Gunther said. "Did you also find the drugs he stole from me?" Asher stared him down and didn't answer. "Do you or the police have them now?"

"The police," Asher said.

Gunther swore. Asher was stalling, she realized, trying to keep Gunther from firing his flare gun and setting the boat on fire until backup arrived. She glanced toward the shore. They were drifting farther and farther away. If the puppies jumped now, they might be able to swim for it. But not if they drifted for much longer.

"Finn stole from me," Gunther said, "so I shot him and left him to die. I didn't care where he crawled off to."

This was all wrong, Peyton thought. Gunther was confessing too easily, and Asher still hadn't pulled his badge. Did Gunther still think he could work with them?

"I gave you the opportunity to prove yourself," Gunther said. "I had my guys put you to work. I asked them to watch you. It's not until I ended up in jail that it finally clicked that somehow I got played and every word you told me is a lie!"

The boat drifted farther away from the shore. Soon there would be no way the dogs would be able to make the swim, even if she could convince them to.

"You really had me fooled," Gunther went on. The malice in his voice made it clear he didn't like to be fooled. "I had you researched. You came up clean. And that's worth even more than the value of what Finn stole. I don't care if you're a dirty cop or a con man, as long as you work for me and do what I say. You owe me a debt that you're going to repay. Good fake IDs for me and my guys. Packages you're going to deliver where I say, when I say, until I decide you and me are square. Otherwise, I'm going to put a target out on your woman and everyone else that you love."

"Let her and the dogs go," Asher said, "and we can go wherever you want and work something out."

"Nah," Gunther snorted. "She matters to you, and as long as I have her, you'll do what I say."

Asher's left hand slipped behind his back. She watched as Asher signaled, using her training hand signals.

*Jump. Run.*

She glanced to the shore.

No. She couldn't just take off and leave Asher. Not on a boat with this madman.

He signaled her again.

*Go!*

Asher glanced back over his shoulder. His eyes met hers, strong and unflinching, and she knew without a doubt what he wanted her to do.

She signaled him back. *Yes.*

Relief filled his eyes. He turned back to Gunther, flashed him a badge and pulled out his weapon.

"No deal," Asher said. "My name is Officer Asher Gilmore of the Pacific Northwest K-9 Unit, and you're under arrest."

Gunther howled and swore in anger.

But Peyton didn't stop to listen. Instead she bent down and scooped the three bloodhounds up into her arms, the best she could, leaving just Spark, who stayed close by his partner's side. Peyton leaped over the edge of the boat. For a moment she tumbled through the air. The puppies wriggled from her grasp. She hit the water and went under. It was so cold it knocked the air from her lungs. She surfaced and gasped a breath.

The three dogs were paddling around her, panicked and uncertain. She glanced back to the boat. She could still hear Asher and Gunther shouting. Everything in her heart ached to leave him. But instead she focused her eyes on the shore.

"Come on!" she ordered the dogs. "Swim!"

Slowly, she began to swim toward the shore, calling to the dogs and coaxing them to follow her. Agent, Ranger and Chief paddled alongside her.

"Spark!" Asher's commanding voice rose. "Jump! Go with Peyton!"

She heard Spark bark and saw his black-and-white form streak through the sky as the dog leaped overboard. Her heart ached to know how hard it would have been for the dog to follow his partner's order and leave Asher. She called to Spark and the dog paddled to her side. The shore grew closer. She felt the muddy ground beneath her feet. She stood and watched, as the dogs swam past her and one by one they scrambled up on the shore to safety.

Then a sudden roar shook the air. Heat rushed toward her. She looked back. *The Mixed Blessing* was engulfed in fire. Smoke billowed over the water. Flames licked up toward the sky.

*Asher!*

Her heart lurched. Smoke stung her eyes. Tears slipped down her cheeks.

*Dear Lord, please save Asher! I need him to be okay.*

Then she saw Asher's strong form leaping from the flames like a phoenix. He dove into the water as smoke and debris rained down around him. She swam for him, pushing her body through the water until she reached him. Asher stood. The water was up to his shoulders. Water streamed down his handsome face.

"Are you okay?" she asked.

"I'm okay," Asher said. "Gunther took the lifeboat, but I'm sure he won't get far."

Asher swept her up into his arms and lifted her up out of the water. She wrapped her arms around his neck. He cradled her against his chest. Their lips met and he kissed her. She kissed him back without fear or worry, knowing the man she'd liked for so long was now the one she was falling in love with.

He carried her back to shore. Spark and the puppies galloped toward them, pressing their muddy bodies up against Asher's legs. Asher set her down on the beach. Her feet touched the ground. But Asher kept one arm draped around her shoulders. She wrapped her arms around his waist. They walked back up the beach as Spark and the bloodhounds scampered around them. The sound of helicopters filled the sky. Lights flashed through the trees from emergency vehicles arriving and surrounding the house.

*Thank You, God.*

Rescue had arrived. It was all over.

Then suddenly she heard a buzzing noise. Asher pulled away from her and got his cell phone from his pocket. It was still in the same waterproof case he'd used for diving.

He looked down at the screen and his eyes widened.

"It's a message from my sister, Mara," Asher said. "She wants me to call her."

Asher stared at his phone. Hope and fear battled for dominance inside his chest.

It had been too long since he'd last heard from his sister. He'd regretted so much about their last communication and had been praying that God would give him the opportunity to make things right and help bring her home.

Was this it? Was the nightmare that they had been living through for six months finally over?

"Go call her," Peyton said.

Her hand brushed his arm. Asher turned toward her. He'd been moments away from telling Peyton that he thought he was falling in love with her and wanted her by his side. And now, here like a splash of cold water to the face, was the reminder that his life had too many dangling threads he had to deal with before he could even consider pledging his heart to someone like Peyton.

"Asher?" Peyton's eyes were on his face, and he realized he still hadn't moved. "Go call Mara. We can talk when you get back."

His screen only showed half a bar of cell service.

"I'm going to try to walk up the hill a bit to get a better signal," Asher said. "Will you wait for me?"

"I'm going to take the puppies straight to the PNK9 and stay with them for a while to help them get settled," Peyton said. "But I won't leave the scene without checking in with you."

Right, the case was over. He assumed Peyton would be going back to the hotel suite at some point to get her stuff. But he wouldn't necessarily be there then, and this might actually be the last time they'd be alone together for a while.

"Okay," he said. "I'll see you in a few minutes."

He turned and walked up the beach and through the trees toward the cottage. Police, park rangers, search and rescue, and PNK9 officers swarmed the scene. He saw Tanner and Britta taking Vaughan and Ridges into custody with the help of Jackson and Rex. He nodded to his fellow officers and they nodded back.

Then he saw Donovan striding toward him with his aging Malinois, Sarge, loping by his side. The chief signaled him over. Asher and Spark jogged over to him.

"Good job," Donovan said with a wide smile. "You really came through for us on this one."

"Thank you, Chief," Asher said. "It was a real team effort. Tanner came through with a strong assist at the end. Jackson was a great help as well. And of course I couldn't have done any of this without Peyton. She really is exceptional."

"She is," Donovan concurred. "I'm very pleased with how well this resolved. The Coast Guard picked up Gunther and has him in custody. His wife, Annika, was devastated to hear of the death of her son and has agreed to testify against Gunther. The three other drug dealers have all been apprehended as well, and the dogs have been rescued." He ran a hand through his thick brown hair. "It's a real win for the team."

If only everything else in life wrapped up that nicely, Asher thought.

"I just got a text from Mara," Asher said, "with a number for me to call. Am I authorized to tell her that we recovered Stacey's diary?"

"Yes," Donovan said reservedly. "You can. But please reinforce the fact that it may end up having no bearing on the ongoing investigation, and our commitment continues to be to making sure whoever killed Stacey and Jonas faces justice."

"Understood," Asher said.

He couldn't begin to imagine the tightrope the chief was walking. Donovan had never weighed in on whether he personally believed in Mara's guilt or innocence, only that he wanted her to come home safely.

Asher and Spark continued up the driveway, past the cottage and the vehicles, until his phone gave him three bars. Then he held his breath and dialed the number.

"Hello?" The voice was female, tentative, but Asher knew instantly that it was his half sister.

He clutched the phone. "It's so good to hear your voice, Mara."

"You too," Mara said. "I don't have much time. Can you do one thing for me? Can you go visit Dad? Please?"

Asher swallowed hard and thought about what Peyton had said.

*Lord, my relationship with Mara is so broken and she doesn't trust me. Help me to step up and be the big brother she needs me to be.*

"I will. He's in a safe house." Asher took a breath. "I just want to say that I'm sorry, for everything. I was dismissive, I didn't listen and I was too focused on doing things my way. We're onto Eli now. Stacey's diary proves they were in conflict, she suspected him. Might not pan out, but we're looking hard."

He heard a small sob.

"I should have trusted you…and the team. I saw Eli shoot Stacey and Jonas," Mara said. "He's been chasing me ever since. He sent me a picture of Dad in his yellow sweater and threatened to kill both him and you. I've been hiding out. I called today because I saw him in Mount Rainier National Park not far from my last hiding place, talking to a shady-looking guy."

He gripped the phone. "I'll come find you. Where are you now?"

She inhaled sharply. Had she detected a threat?

Her voice dropped to barely above a whisper. "Dad's favorite place."

The call suddenly went dead. He redialed, but the call didn't go through. Still he stood there for a long moment and stared at the phone.

Then he and Spark walked back toward the light and the noise of law enforcement to find

Peyton. Before he'd even reached the cottage, he saw her walking toward him with the three bloodhounds in tow.

Her eyes met his, and as he searched her face, he could feel his heart splintering inside him. He wanted to pull her into his arms, tell her how much she meant to him and promise he'd love and cherish her forever. But he wasn't ready. Not yet. He had to go find his sister and meet with his father. He didn't know how that would shake him, and Peyton deserved someone who was completely ready to devote his life to her.

"How's Mara?" she asked.

"She's okay—alive and in hiding," Asher said. "Mara says she witnessed Eli murder Stacey and Jonas. She's been on the run from him ever since. He threatened to murder both Dad and me. She wants me to go visit our dad to make sure he's okay. I just wish I'd handled this whole thing differently from the beginning. Then maybe she'd have trusted me enough to tell me all this before."

Peyton stepped toward him. He watched as her hands opened as if to reach for him, and he could feel his own arms wanting to open for her in response. But instead he held back and slid his hands in his pockets.

"I don't quite know how to say this," he said,

"but I think I need to take a break from the PNK9 to focus on my family. I told Mara I'd come find her. Plus I've got to go talk to Dad. And I don't know how long all that's going to take and how it's going to affect me. But I'm done letting my personal issues impact the team, and I think I need some time to figure it out."

Just like that, he watched as her face fell and the light dimmed in her eyes. Something in his heart hoped she'd throw her arms around his neck and ask him to stay. Instead, Peyton nodded.

"I think that's smart," she said. "You need to do that, and I need to focus on assessing and rehabilitating the pups."

"I know if anyone can get them back on the right track you can," Asher said.

"Thank you," she said. "It was fun to be out in the field, but it's time I get back to leading the kennels and training the dogs."

"Yeah, I think so too," Asher said. A faint smile crossed his lips. "For what it's worth, I never thought of you as a sidekick. You're a leader, Peyton. You're an incredible trainer and any person who doesn't see that in you is wrong."

She nodded without responding.

"Good night, Peyton," he said.

"Good night, Asher."

But still neither of them moved or turned to walk away. Instead, they both stood there, locked on each other's gaze. He watched as conflicting emotions danced in her eyes, and he was sure his own face looked every bit as conflicted as well.

*Lord, saying goodbye to this woman is the hardest thing I've ever had to do. Help me have the courage to step up and be the man I need to be.*

Then finally they both turned and walked away.

# FOURTEEN

The late afternoon sunlight streamed through the windows of the PNK9 training center, casting the room in a gentle orange glow. Peyton was on one knee in one of the pens with Ranger, Agent and Chief, running them through a search drill.

It had been five days since they'd been rescued from the dingy basement, and already she was beginning to see the joy returning to their eyes. The PNK9 vet had given them a clean bill of health, except for some minor cuts and bruises. Agent had a slight sprain to one of his front paws but was already back to running on it as normal. It was still early days, but already she had hope that they would be able to return to full training and be able to take their place in the field alongside their brothers and sisters in the K-9 family.

*Lord, I feel like my heart is filled with end-*

*less praise and thanksgiving that we found them and brought them safely home.*

True to his word, as soon as Asher had wrapped up the case and had a complete debrief with Donovan, he'd officially taken leave from the PNK9. She hadn't seen him since they'd said good-night back at the crime scene in the woods, and she didn't know when she'd ever see him again. But although her heart had missed him every single day, as if a piece of her was missing, ever since the case something inside her had felt stronger and more certain too.

Ranger began to howl, and within moments Agent and Chief joined him. The three dogs scampered over to the gate of the pen. Someone was coming down the hall. She stood and ran her hands down her legs.

Spark galloped down the hallway toward her. A laugh slipped her lips, and she opened the pen door to welcome him in. Spark licked her hand and then sniffed around the bloodhounds in a flurry of wagging tails.

Hope alighted in her heart.

Was Asher here?

Then she saw him. His handsome form was back in his crisp PNK9 uniform. His face was clean-shaven again, showing the strong lines of his jaw, and his hair had been trimmed. But even more than that, there was something different in his eyes as well. He carried himself with a confidence and a certainty that seemed to radiate through him.

Then she spotted the bouquet of roses in his hand.

She slipped out of the pen and closed the door behind her, leaving Spark to play with the bloodhounds.

"Hey, Peyton," he said. His cheeks reddened slightly. "I don't know if the fact you said you liked roses was just part of your cover, but I remembered and so I got them for you."

He held out the flowers like a teenager offering his date a corsage.

"I love them," she said. "Thank you."

As she took the flowers, her fingertips touched his and she felt electricity sizzle through them.

"I missed you," Asher said.

"I missed you too," she admitted. "Does this mean you're back?"

"Back to stay," he said with a smile. "It's been a pretty overwhelming few days. I went to visit my dad at the PNK9 safe house. It was good, but it wasn't easy. He was so old and frail. Not at all like the confident man I remember him being. Trying to talk to him was like listening to a broken record on loop. The moments he did remember me, he thought I was about eleven or twelve."

Her chest ached for how hard it must've been for him.

"I have so much respect for you for going through that," Peyton said.

"I told him that I'd come back to visit him once a week," Asher said. "I need to let go of the man he used to be and be there for him now."

"I'm sure Mara will be happy to hear that," she said.

"Mara said she was in Dad's favorite spot," Asher said. "I'm guessing she was afraid of being overheard. But I talked to Dad about his camping memories and it helped me narrow down where she could be. I was originally planning on taking Spark and going to look for her. But when I talked to the chief, he authorized a rescue mission. He sent Tanner and Britta. Britta is very skilled in tracking people and Tanner is such a strong officer. I know Mara couldn't possibly be in better care."

"I hope he finds her and brings her home soon," Peyton said.

"Me too," Asher said. "Congratulations on the dogs. I hear they got a clean bill of health and they're doing well."

"They are," Peyton said. "Congrats on all

your work in closing up our case. I heard both Annika and Vaughan have already pled guilty to drug smuggling and racketeering in exchange for cooperation, and charges have been filed against Gunther, Laurence and Ridges as well."

"With Vaughan, he just saw which way the wind was blowing and decided to turn on the others while a lighter sentence was still on the table," Asher said. "But it seems Annika actually wasn't involved in Gunther's smuggling business and she tried to turn a blind eye to it."

"Until her son, Finn, disappeared and she suspected he was dead," Peyton said.

"Right," Asher said. "The police wouldn't help her and Gunther was lying to her. So when she saw someone had tried to kill us while we were scuba diving, she smelled something was up. I honestly don't know if she had any idea we were law enforcement or just suspected we might be rival drug dealers. Either way, she took the huge risk of telling us that Finn loved Lake Crescent in the hopes we'd succeed in doing what she didn't and find her son's body."

Which they had.

"On a happy note, I heard from Ember," Peyton said. "She's still in Portland and doing well."

"I'm glad to hear that," Asher said.

"Looks like the adventures of Dan and Merry Johnson have finally come to a close and been all wrapped up," Peyton said, "with no loose threads."

"There is one loose thread," Asher said.

He reached for her hand and took it. His thumb traced over her fingers.

"The whole time we were undercover as 'Dan and Merry' I couldn't come up with the right nickname for you," Asher said. "Because the only word that ever felt right was when I called you my wife. I've fallen in love with you, Peyton. I want our life together to be for real. I want our backyard wedding and a home together with half a dozen kids. I want to have your back as you chase your professional dreams, and I want to build my life with you."

Tears filled her eyes. "I want that too."

"I love you, Peyton."

"I love you too," she said. "I've had a crush on you ever since the day you first walked into the kennels, and you're the only man I could ever imagine spending my life with."

Asher wrapped his arms around her waist. She threw both arms around his neck, still holding the roses in one hand.

"Will you marry me?" Hope filled his green eyes.

"I will."

Then she stood up on her tiptoes and kissed his smiling mouth. He kissed her back, and they stood there, with their arms wrapped around each other as Spark and the three bloodhounds barked and howled happily.

\* \* \* \* \*

*Don't miss Tanner Ford and Mara Gilmore's story,* Snowbound Escape, *and the rest of the Pacific Northwest K-9 Unit series:*

Dear Reader,

Last summer, I drove all by myself down the Eastern US coast and back, with stops in New York, Pennsylvania, Maryland, Virginia, West Virginia, North Carolina, South Carolina, Georgia and Florida. I returned with my heart full of stories of the people I met along the way.

Emma, who was visiting Texas, found me a pair of shorts when I sat in gum. Lamont in Maryland had an emergency fix for my laptop. A customer service rep in Florida was endlessly patient when my Canadian credit card wouldn't work. A precocious two-and-a-half-year-old named Margaret regaled me with stories on a bus trip. A manager outside Pittsburgh gave me a free breakfast and took a copy of one of my books for his wife. Time and again, waitstaff greeted me with a smile after a long day's drive. And there were so many more.

This book is for them and everyone who takes that extra moment out of their day to make somebody else's day brighter, even when nobody notices the work you do. As always, thank you again for sharing this journey with me.

*Maggie*

# Get 3 FREE REWARDS!

## We'll send you 2 FREE Books plus a FREE Mystery Gift.

**FREE**
Value Over
**$20**

Both the **Love Inspired®** and **Love Inspired® Suspense** series feature compelling novels filled with inspirational romance, faith, forgiveness and hope.

---

**YES!** Please send me 2 FREE novels from the Love Inspired or Love Inspired Suspense series and my FREE gift (gift is worth about $10 retail). After receiving them, if I don't wish to receive any more books, I can return the shipping statement marked "cancel." If I don't cancel, I will receive 6 brand-new Love Inspired Larger-Print books or Love Inspired Suspense Larger-Print books every month and be billed just $6.49 each in the U.S. or $6.74 each in Canada. That is a savings of at least 16% off the cover price. It's quite a bargain! Shipping and handling is just 50¢ per book in the U.S. and $1.25 per book in Canada.* I understand that accepting the 2 free books and gift places me under no obligation to buy anything. I can always return a shipment and cancel at any time by calling the number below. The free books and gift are mine to keep no matter what I decide.

Choose one:  ☐ **Love Inspired**        ☐ **Love Inspired**        ☐ **Or Try Both!**
                      **Larger-Print**             **Suspense**                  (122/322 & 107/307
                      (122/322 BPA GRPA)      **Larger-Print**              BPA GRRP)
                                                        (107/307 BPA GRPA)

---

Name (please print)

---

Address                                                                                          Apt. #

---

City                                        State/Province                                Zip/Postal Code

---

**Email:** Please check this box ☐ if you would like to receive newsletters and promotional emails from Harlequin Enterprises ULC and its affiliates. You can unsubscribe anytime.

### Mail to the Harlequin Reader Service:
**IN U.S.A.:** P.O. Box 1341, Buffalo, NY 14240-8531
**IN CANADA:** P.O. Box 603, Fort Erie, Ontario L2A 5X3

Want to try 2 free books from another series? Call 1-800-873-8635 or visit www.ReaderService.com.

LIRLIS23

# HARLEQUIN
## PLUS

Try the best multimedia
subscription service for romance
readers like you!

## **Read, Watch and Play.**

Experience the easiest way to get
the romance content you crave.

Start your **FREE TRIAL** at
<u>www.harlequinplus.com/freetrial</u>.